NEW YORK NIGHT LIFE

"Listen," Canyon O'Grady told the two men in his hotel room, "I'm tired. I'm kicking you out of here."

The one called Boyle got a kick out of this. His ugly face broke into an ugly grin. But the other one said, "Stop fooling around, Boyle. Let's kill him and get out of here."

His hand held the .32 he had taken off Canyon. Meanwhile Boyle casually hefted O'Grady's .44.

All Canyon had was the knife he buried in Boyle's belly. Boyle screamed. O'Grady grabbed the .44 from his hand, and hit the floor. A slug from the .32 punched into Canyon's shoulder as his blast took the second man in the stomach.

This was Canyon O'Grady's first night in New York, where frontier justice yielded to the law of the jungle, and the only wide-open spaces were bullet holes.

CANYON O'GRADY

18

BLOOD BOUNTY

by
Jon Sharpe

A SIGNET BOOK

SIGNET
Published by the Penguin Group
Penguin Books USA Inc., 375 Hudson Street,
New York, New York, 10014, U.S.A.
Penguin Books Ltd, 27 Wrights Lane, London W8 5TZ, England
Penguin Books Australia Ltd, Ringwood, Victoria, Australia
Penguin Books Canada Ltd, 10 Alcorn Avenue, Toronto, Ontario, Canada M4V 3B2
Penguin Books (N.Z.) Ltd, 182-190 Wairau Road,
Auckland 10, New Zealand

Penguin Books Ltd, Registered Offices:
Harmondsworth, Middlesex, England

First published by Signet,
an imprint of New American Library,
a division of Penguin Books USA Inc.

First Printing, March, 1992

10 9 8 7 6 5 4 3 2 1

Canyon O'Grady

His was a heritage of blackguards and poets, fighters and lovers, men who could draw a pistol and bed a lass with the same ease.

Freedom was a cry seared into Canyon O'Grady, justice a banner of the heart.

With the great wave of those who fled to America, the new land of hope and heartbreak, solace and savagery, he came to ride the untamed wilderness of the Old West.

With a smile or a six-gun, Canyon O'Grady became a name feared by some and welcomed by others but remembered by all . . .

*April, 1862, on the Kansas plains,
where the law was something a man
made for himself, and the quality
of his handiwork spelled out
the difference between life and death . . .*

1

When Canyon O'Grady rode into the town of West Bend, Kansas, it was in response to a request from his old friend Del Locken. The two men had known each other many years, and although a long interval had passed between their early friendship and the present, Canyon still considered Locken one of his oldest friends. Hell, the mere fact that they had gone their separate ways as young men, and had both subsequently ended up as agents for the United States Secret Service, showed just how much alike they really were.

Canyon expected to find his friend hale and hearty and ready to explain the summons. Instead, Del Locken was lying facedown in the undertaker's office with three clean pink bullet holes in his back.

Canyon had tried the hotel first, and then several saloons, but each time he asked for Locken people gave him odd looks and shrugs and nothing more. He finally went to the Sheriff, who directed him to the undertaker's office.

Canyon didn't really need to turn the head of the dead man and look at the face, but he did so anyway. He saw Del Locken's lifeless features and was shocked.

He couldn't remember ever having seen Locken without a smile on his face.

Canyon turned to the undertaker and asked, "Do you know who shot him?"

"Didn't the Sheriff tell you?" the man asked.

"The Sheriff told me as little as he could."

"That don't surprise me," the undertaker said.

The name outside the door said Elias Leech, and Mr. Leech looked like anything but what he was. A pudgy, pink-skinned man, he had soft, full lips.

"I shouldn't say," Leech told Canyon, "but it was the Moler boys."

"What's their claim?" Canyon asked.

"They're just mean," Leech said.

"Would they have done this for no good reason?"

"Chances are they was paid," Leech said, "but you didn't hear it from me."

"Thanks. I'll take it up with the Sheriff."

As Canyon headed for the door Leech said, "I guess you and this fella were friends."

At the door Canyon turned and said, "We were."

"He have any kin?"

"No," the agent said, "none."

"Sheriff's got his personal effects," Leech said. "Don't let him tell you he didn't."

The undertaker, Elias Leech, was the only person in town who had treated Canyon with any courtesy up to this point. Maybe the fact that the man was an undertaker made his helpfulness surprising. But, hell, Canyon reflected, it was a job that somebody had to do, and no reason why a decent man couldn't be doing it.

"I'm grateful," Canyon said. "I'll be paying for the burial."

"Anything fancy?" Leech asked.

"No," Canyon said, "nothing fancy."

When Canyon O'Grady walked into the office of the Sheriff of West Bend for the second time that day, the man looked up from his desk.

"Saw your friend, did ya?" Sheriff Ben Tower asked.

"I did. What can you tell me about the men who shot him?"

"The Molers?" Tower asked. "What about them?"

"Well, for one thing," Canyon said, "why aren't they in jail for backshooting a man?"

"There's three of 'em," Tower said, as if that explained it all—and to this man, maybe it did. Tower was in his late forties, and probably looked at his job as a nice, quiet way to pass the time.

"And I ain't got any deputies," Tower added.

"You do now."

"Huh?"

"I've just sworn myself in," Canyon said. "Give me a badge."

Sheriff Tower looked as if he wanted to protest, but he decided not to. He opened the top drawer of his desk on the right side, extracted a deputy sheriff's badge, and tossed it to Canyon, who caught it neatly with one hand.

He pinned it on his jacket and said, "Now, after I've killed them, you won't be tempted to come after me because I'm only one man."

"I wouldn't—" Tower said, and then just stopped and stared at Canyon.

As the Secret Service agent started for the door Tower got brave and called out. "How come you just happened to ride into town the same day he got shot?"

"I was coming here to meet him today."

"I guess you was too late, huh?"

"No, Sheriff," Canyon O'Grady said over his shoulder, "I got here just in time."

West Bend had one saloon, the Oasis. It was near the hotel. Canyon stopped outside it and looked up and down the street. He wondered if the streets were always this empty, or if the townspeople simply realized that the shooting wasn't all done yet.

When Canyon entered the saloon, there was only one man seated at a table, nursing a beer. The man paid him no mind as he walked to the bar. Canyon ordered a whiskey, and the barkeep's hand shook as he poured it. The agent put his money on the bar, and as the man moved to take it Canyon caught a skinny wrist in a tight grip. If he squeezed, he'd rub thin bones together painfully.

"The Moler brothers," he said in a low voice.

The bartender replied without hesitation.

"That's one, behind you."

"And the others?"

"Upstairs."

"Doing what?"

"Whatever they do upstairs."

Canyon studied the man's frightened features for a few more seconds, then released his wrist and said, "Get out."

The bartender did not have to be told twice.

Canyon drank his whiskey and then turned to face the first Moler.

"Which one are you?" he asked.

Moler looked up, and Canyon noticed that the man had the largest ears he had ever seen.

"I'm Virgil. What's it to you?"

"You killed a friend of my mine today."

"Did I, now?"

"You and your brothers."

"We backshot something today," Virgil Moler admitted, "but that warn't no man. That was a no-account bounty hunter."

"He was no bounty hunter," Canyon said, "and his name was Locken."

"And I suppose you ain't no bounty hunter neither, right?"

"That's right, Moler," Canyon said, "I'm the law."

Moler laughed.

"That badge don't mean nothin' to me, mister. If you was a friend of that bounty hunter, then you must be a no-good bounty hunter too."

"I'm no bounty hunter," Canyon said.

"Then what are you doing here?"

"I'm here to dispense justice, Moler."

"That mean you want to kill me?"

"It does."

"And my brothers, too?"

"That's right."

"Well," Virgil Moler said, standing up, "I guess you got to start somewheres."

Virgil Moler was a fool, that much was plain. First he backshot a man, then he admitted it, and now he was spreading his legs, readying himself for a fair draw that would never come. While he was adjusting his legs Canyon simply drew his gun and fired.

Wide-eyed, the dying man stood there and said, "That warn't fair."

As the man fell Canyon did not dignify the remark with an answer.

Starting up the stairs, he ejected the spent load and pushed in a fresh round. He went up the steps slowly. He had no way of knowing if the other two Molers had heard the shot, and if they had, how they would react. It was likely they'd figure it was their brother, having some fun.

When he reached the second flood, he paused to listen. He heard the sounds men make when they're doing what men do on the second floor of a saloon. He started down the hall, moving cautiously, on the lookout for loose or creaking floorboards. By this time a man was moaning aloud and a woman was making a high-pitched keening sound as if she were about to die. One of the brothers was getting real close to finishing his good time.

He didn't know how close.

Canyon found the door that the sounds were coming from. He held his gun in his right hand, braced his back against the opposite wall, and kicked the door open.

On the bed he saw a man's bare ass and a woman's legs and thighs wrapped around him. The man turned and stared over his shoulder, his mouth slack. The girl beneath him leaned sideways to look also.

"What the—" the man said.

"Just stay where you are," Canyon said, showing them both his gun.

"What do you want?" the man asked.

Canyon moved into the room and to the side to get a better look at the man's face. As he did he saw the ears on the man and he now figured that these were the Moler trademark.

"Which Moler are you?"

"I'm Matt. Who are you?"

"I'm the man who just killed Virgil."

"W-what? That shot?"

"That's right."

"You killed my brother?"

"And you're next."

The man's eyes bugged out and he said, "You can't shoot me like this!"

The woman beneath him began to whimper.

Canyon saw the man's gunbelt hanging on the bedpost and said, "There's your gun."

Matt Moler licked his lips and eyed his gun, but at that moment another man entered the room, half naked and talking.

"Jesus, Matt, what are ya doin' to the bitch—"

"Mike, look out! This son of a bitch just killed Virgil!"

Unarmed, the man took one look at Canyon and backed out of the room. The agent could hear him pounding down the hall, no doubt after a gun.

Meanwhile, the man on the bed had disengaged himself from the woman and was groping for his gun. Canyon wasted no time. He fired once, catching Moler in the back of the head, and the man fell heavily onto the woman beneath him, who hadn't managed to slither away in time.

She started screaming as blood and brains spattered her naked body.

Canyon backed up quickly, pressing his back to the wall, and waited. The third Moler had to have his gun by now, and he was either long gone, or waiting in the hall.

The woman on the bed was still screaming, so Canyon pointed his gun at her and yelled, "Shut up!" She fell silent, except for an occasional sob.

Quickly, Canyon moved past the bed to the window to look outside. It was a sheer drop to the street below. He moved back to the wall and listened intently.

"Mike, what's happenin'—" a woman said, and Mike Moler shouted, "get back inside!"

Both voices came from the hall.

Canyon jumped out into the hallway, keeping himself low. Sure enough, Moler was there, right in the middle of the hall. Moler—and there were those ears again—started to bring his gun to bear, but Canyon was quicker. The agent shot the man square in the chest. The man's back had just hit the floor when Canyon straddled him, standing over him.

"Why'd you kill Locken?" he demanded.

Mike Moler opened his mouth to reply and a pink bubble formed and then exploded.

"Jesus—" Moler gasped.

"Why, Moler?"

"P-paid to . . ."

"By who?"

"M-man . . ." Moler said. "Called himself the . . . Duke. Said bounty hunter was trailin' him . . . paid us to . . . to . . . Jesus, mister, it hurts!"

As the light in the man's eyes went out Canyon O'Grady said, "Not anymore it doesn't."

2

Canyon entered the sheriff's office for the third time that day and tossed the deputy's badge onto the man's desk. It bounced, and the sheriff reacted as if it were hot, jerking away from it.

"It's over?" he said.

"It's over, Sheriff," Canyon said.

"They're all dead?" Tower asked. "All of the Molers?"

"All of them. You had better get someone over there to clean up mess. You are the garbageman around here, too, aren't you?"

"I, uh, guess—"

"Is there paper on the Moler boys, Sheriff?"

"Wanted posters?" the sheriff said. "Uh, no, there ain't."

"So the only reason they might go after a man they thought was a bounty hunter was if someone paid them. Am I right?"

"Bein' paid was the only reason the Moler boys ever had for movin'," Tower said.

"Mike Moler said they were hired by a man who called himself the Duke. You ever hear of this man?"

"The Duke?" the sheriff repeated, shaking his head.

"He's not from around here. Must've been passin' through."

"And you walk around strangers in this town, don't you, Sheriff?"

The lawman looked away.

"How'd you get that badge, anyway," Canyon asked. "Nobody else wanted it?"

Tower looked at him. "How did you know?"

"It was a safe bet," Canyon said. "I want Locken's personal effects."

"Uh, the undertaker's got them. Ask him."

Canyon leaned on the man's desk and said, "I'm asking you."

The sheriff swallowed and opened a desk drawer.

Canyon went to the hotel and got Locken's key from the clerk. In Locken's room he looked around, but there was nothing there but some extra shirts, an extra gun, and some bullets.

He sat on the bed and looked at the stuff he'd gotten from the sheriff. Some money in a wallet—there'd probably been more, but the sheriff had likely spent it—a letter to someone named Jane, which he hadn't mailed yet—Canyon didn't know who Jane was—and an old knife which Canyon recognized. Locken'd had that knife a long time, and the blade had dulled over the years. He'd only kept it as a lucky piece.

Canyon dropped the knife and picked the wallet up from the bed. He riffled through it and found a folded-up piece of paper. He unfolded it and spread it out. It was a letter addressed to Canyon, but obviously never mailed. Maybe Locken had meant to leave it behind for Canyon to find. It was brief, saying only that Locken was on the trail of a man called the Duke. The letter also said that Locken was sorry he'd made Canyon come all the way to West Bend, but that he had decided that finding the Duke was his job alone. He hoped that Canyon would understand.

For some reason Locken had wanted to be sure he got this man by himself. Now he wouldn't be able to get him at all.

I'll get him for you, Del, Canyon vowed silently.

But where should he start? That question was answered as he continued to go through the wallet. He found a railroad ticket, final destination New York City.

By the time Canyon left the hotel carrying his gear, the Moler brothers had been removed from the saloon. He stopped at the sheriff's office on his way to the livery. This was the fourth and final visit.

"You clean up real quick," he said to the sheriff.

"Yeah," Tower said. He was pouring himself a cup of coffee and didn't offer Canyon one.

"Did you check out the Moler boys?" Canyon asked.

"Uh, what do you mean . . . check them out?"

"Don't play dense with me, Sheriff," Canyon said. "How much money did they have on them?"

"Uh, they each had more than one hundred dollars on them."

"One hundred dollars?" Canyon asked. "Are they local?"

"Yeah."

"How long would it take them to earn that kind of money in this town?"

Sheriff Tower laughed. "In a week, a month, or a year?"

"Where's the money now?"

Very quickly the sheriff's eyes went to the desk and then away.

"I . . . guess it's at the undertaker's—"

Canyon walked around behind the desk and started opening drawers.

"Hey, you can't do that—"

"You going to stop me?"

The sheriff took one step forward, then stopped and took two steps back, shaking his head in disgust.

Canyon found the money in a drawer and took it out. There was over five hundred dollars there. He counted out enough for four burials and dropped it on the desk.

"I'll be back to see the graves," he said.

The sheriff hesitated a moment, then licked his lips and said, "They'll be there."

Canyon tucked the rest of the money into his pocket and walked out. He went to the livery, retrieved his horse, Cormac, and rode out of town. He had to find the nearest railroad station and start his journey to New York City.

3

On the train Canyon O'Grady thought about the man Del Locken had been chasing. With a name like the Duke, Canyon was surprised that he hadn't heard of the man before. He wondered if Locken was after him for personal or professional reasons. Canyon would have to wait to find out until he telegraphed Washington from New York. He hadn't already sent a message to his superior, Major General Rufus Wheeler, because he was afraid the man might order him back to Washington. Better to send the message once he was already in New York.

He wondered why Locken had summoned him to West Bend and then changed his mind. For Locken to ask for help in the beginning he must have figured that this Duke character would be hard to take alone.

That bothered Canyon. Del Locken was one of the toughest men he'd ever known, and he'd been taken the only way a man like him *could* be taken . . . from behind.

And that was the true reason that Canyon O'Grady was on his way to New York. It wasn't so much the fact that Locken had been killed as the way he'd been killed.

The Moler brothers had pulled the trigger, but the odds said that the Duke had paid them to do it.

As the train pulled into the station Canyon grabbed his bag. The trip had been planned—if that word could be used—on the spur of the moment, and he didn't have much in the way of gear with him. He had his gun, his rifle, and some extra clothes, and that was all.

As the train began to discharge passengers at the station Canyon found himself in the middle of a pressing crowd. He'd never before seen so many people in one place at one time, all trying to fit into the same space.

Being jostled did not sit well with him, so he broke free as soon as he could.

"Need a cab, sir?" a voice asked.

He turned and saw a man standing nearby.

"What?"

"A ride?" the man said. "Do you need a ride somewhere?"

"Yeah, sure," Canyon said.

"This way."

He followed the man to a horse-drawn cab, similar to ones he had seen in Washington, D.C. and other cities.

"Get in."

Canyon hesitated.

"You're from the West, aren't you?" the man asked. He was young, in his twenties, and very slim, with a shock of unkempt brown hair.

"Good guess."

"You're gonna need some clothes."

"Clothes?"

"Unless you want to attract attention every time you walk down the street."

"Do you know where I can get some?"

"Sure."

"Cheap?"

"Well . . . let's say inexpensive."

"And then a hotel to match?"

"I know just the place."

"All right," Canyon said, "let's go."

Using the money generously donated by the Moler boys—the Duke's money—Canyon bought himself two suits of clothes more suitable for New York.

"Here's the hotel," his driver said.

Canyon looked outside.

"It doesn't look inexpensive."

"Take my word for it," his driver said. "There are hotels much more expensive than this in this city."

That still didn't make this one cheap, but Canyon decided not to argue. After all, it was the Duke's money.

"Okay," he said, getting out of the cab. He grabbed his bag and his rifle and looked at the driver.

"I think you're also gonna need a different gun," the driver said.

"What makes you say that?"

The man smiled.

"You gonna wear those new clothes with that gun on your hip?"

Canyon looked down at the gun in his holster, his .44 Colt.

"I see what you mean," he said. "I suppose you can get me a gun, too?"

"Mister, in this city I can get you anything. You want a woman?"

"I'll get my own women, thanks," Canyon said. "It's not something I usually have a problem with."

The driver looked Canyon up and down and said, "No, I guess not."

"This gun you can get me, would it be a decent one?"

"Hell, a good one."

"How much?"

The cabdriver thought a moment.

"I'll tell you what," he said finally. "A hundred dollars. The ride, the gun, everything."

Canyon studied the man's eyes.

"If I give you a hundred dollars—"

"Don't worry," the man said. "My name's Billy Rosewood. Ask anybody in New York. I'm reliable."

"Reliable," Canyon repeated.

Rosewood nodded.

Canyon took out Locken's lucky knife and asked, "Will you get this sharpened for me, too?"

Rosewood grinned and took it.

"Sure, no extra charge."

"Okay," Canyon said. He gave Billy Rosewood a hundred dollars, knowing he might be kissing it good-bye.

What the hell—it wasn't his money.

He checked into the hotel and found the room rate prohibitive, but he took it anyway. Again he justified the cost by recalling that he was not spending all of his own money. However, at the rate that he was spending the money he'd got from the Moler brothers, it wouldn't be long before he was.

He was pleasantly surprised, however, when he saw the room. It was almost worth the price just for the bathtub, which he made immediate use of. He was drying himself when there was a knock on the door. He wrapped the thick towel around his waist and opened the door.

It was Rosewood.

"You're a fast worker," Canyon said, admitting him.

"The fastest in New York," Rosewood said, sliding past him. "Remember that while you're here."

"What have you got for me?"

"Here."

From inside his jacket Rosewood took out a leather shoulder rig with a gun in the holster. He removed the gun and showed it to Canyon.

"It's a Model 1862 Police Pistol, thirty-six caliber, with a four and a half inch barrel. It won't make much of a bulge, if it makes any at all."

Canyon took the gun and hefted it.

"It holds five shots," Rosewood said. "I can get you a twenty-two caliber gun that holds seven shots, if you like."

"No, this is fine," Canyon said. "If five shots doesn't do it, I don't think two extra would matter."

He checked to see that the gun was fully loaded, and then put it down on the dresser.

"Here," Rosewood said, handing him the shoulder rig, "no extra charge."

"I'm touched by your generosity, Billy," Canyon said, accepting it.

"I'm not so generous, really," Rosewood said. "I figure if you're gonna be here awhile I might get some repeat business."

"Well, I will need someone to show me around."

"I'm your man. You know how to put that thing on?" he asked, indicating the shoulder holster.

"I'll figure it out."

"Anything else I can do for you now?"

"Not today," Canyon said. "I'm going to walk around a bit, find a telegraph office and a decent restaurant."

"Well, don't eat in the hotel dining room. There's a restaurant two blocks west that makes a pretty good steak dinner."

"Thanks."

"Three blocks to the east, and then a block north, you'll find a telegraph office."

"Well," Canyon said, "that's all I need for now."

"If you had more money to spend and were stayin' in a better hotel, there'd be a telegraph line right in the hotel itself."

"I'll remember that next time I'm here. Can you meet me out front at nine in the morning?"

"Nine sharp," Rosewood ssaid. "I'll be there."

"See you then. I'll buy you breakfast."

"You got a deal," Rosewood said, and started for the door. "Oh, I almost forgot."

From his belt he took Locken's lucky knife.

"Got you a real nice edge on this," he said, handing it to Canyon. "Why'd you let it get so dull?"

"It belonged to a friend of mine," Canyon told him. "He carried it only for luck."

"I presume he's dead?"

"Yes."

"Well, with an edge like that on it, you should have more luck with it than he did."

"I hope so."

"See you in the mornin'."

"Right."

Rosewood left and Canyon got dressed. He slipped on the shoulder holster and then slid the gun into it. It was uncomfortable, but he'd get used to it.

He put on one of the suits he'd just bought and checked himself in the mirror. The gun was nestled beneath his arm and hardly showed at all. It would take a tailor's expert eye to catch it.

Satisfied, he left the room to take his little get-acquainted-with-New-York walk.

4

Canyon found the restaurant Rosewood had told him about and had a very satisfying meal of steak, onions, potatoes, and biscuits before continuing on to the telegraph office. It was right where Rosewood had said it would be, on the corner of Fifth Avenue and Twenty-fifth Street.

Inside the office he composed his telegraph message to Major General Rufus Wheeler very carefully. He told him where he was and why, and what information he was looking for—namely, what Del Locken had been working on, and whatever Wheeler had on someone called the Duke.

He paid the check, watched while the message was sent, then told the man what hotel he was in and asked that the answer be run over there.

Canyon walked the streets of New York, stopping in at a bar whenever the urge struck him, having a beer, watching the people. They were dressed differently from the people he saw in western towns, more like the people he saw when he was in San Francisco or St. Louis. Inside a saloon, though, people are people. He saw two men fighting over a barmaid in one saloon, and he saw four men playing poker in another. In still a third he watched as the girls worked the room, teasing the customers, getting them to buy more drinks.

In the last place he stopped at there were three girls working. They were all pretty, all under twenty-five. One was dark-haired and two were blonde. If he had been interested he would have chosen the dark-haired girl, but he was tired from his long trip, and decided that it was time to go back to the hotel and turn in.

Canyon opened his eyes abruptly, staring up in the darkness of the room. Something had awakened him, and he wasn't sure what. He lay still and listened, and finally heard it. Someone was trying to get the door to his room open.

He sat up in bed. The new gun, the .36 Police Model, was on the night table, but he took his .44 from the holster on the bedpost and moved to the door with the weapon. He stood off to one side. When the door opened, he would be behind it.

He waited and waited while someone struggled with the door, becoming almost impatient enough to just fling it open himself, but finally he heard a click and the door opened slightly. He braced himself, waiting. As the door opened wider and wider a strip of light shone into the room, and in that strip he saw a shadow. He waited until the door was opened more than halfway, then slammed into it with his shoulder. He heard the satisfying sound of a man's cry of pain. He opened the door again and discovered that he'd made a mistake— and his discovery came the hard way.

There were two of them.

The one he'd hit with the door was sitting on his butt in the hall, his nose all bloody. The second man did not hesitate. He reached out to grab Canyon's gun with one hand and punched him in the face with the other. Surprised, Canyon yelled out, staggered back, and fell to the floor.

His nose hurt, but he figured he deserved the pain for being so stupid. He had allowed the fact that he was newly arrived in town to lull him into a false sense of security. Anyway, the pain was good. It would keep him alert.

The man who had hit him stepped into the room, and he was a big man—looking even bigger from Canyon's vantage point on the floor. He turned up the gas on the wall lamp, then turned and covered Canyon with his own gun, the .44.

"All right," the big man said, "get up."

Canyon wasn't sure whether the big man was talking to him or his partner, who was still sitting out in the hall. Whatever the case, they both got to their feet.

"You," the bigger man said to Canyon, "sit on the bed."

Canyon did as he was told, he sat on his bed and looked at the .36 Police Model from the corner of his eye. If he could only reach it . . .

"Get the other gun," the big man told his bloody-faced partner.

"Lemme kill 'im," the other man said, still holding one hand to his bloody nose. His voice had a decided nasal quality to it.

"Just do what I tell you, for Chrissake!" the big man said.

"Whataya so peeved at me for?" the smaller man asked.

"You said you could open the door."

"I opened it, didn't I?"

"And you just about woke the whole hotel doin' it," the bigger man said.

"He's right," Canyon said, feeling his nose to see if it was broken. It wasn't, but it was swollen, giving *his* voice a decidedly nasal twang too. "You did do a lousy job."

"Shut up!" they both told him in unison.

"You guys want something?"

"Sure we want somethin', friend," the big man said.

"Good," Canyon said. "Then maybe you can tell me what that is?"

"You."

"Me? Why?"

" 'Cause you're the guy."

Another mistake on Canyon's part. It made sense that this Duke fellow would have the train station covered. These men had obviously been watching and, armed with Locken's description, had picked him out as Locken. Aside from hair color, he and Locken were about the same build and height. If the two men didn't let Canyon's red hair throw them—and obviously they hadn't—they'd assume that he was Locken.

Canyon looked at the second man. He was standing nearby, holding the shoulder rig with the .36 in it. He hadn't bothered to remove the gun from the leather.

"Why me?" Canyon asked again. "What do you mean, I'm the guy?"

The gun in the big man's hand was now held negligently. It was no longer pointing directly at Canyon, but at some space between them.

"Listen," Canyon said, "I'm tired, and I'm getting impatient. In a minute I'm going to kick both of you right out of here."

The second man laughed. His nosebleed had stopped, but his nose might well be broken.

"Did you hear him, Boyle? He's gonna kick you outa here." The man looked at Canyon and said, "Go ahead, kick Boyle outa here. That I gotta see."

"How do you think you're gonna do that, Locken?" the big man, Boyle, asked. "We got your guns."

"Oh, I see the mistake now," Canyon said.

"Somebody make a mistake?" Boyle asked.

"You did, if you think my name is Locken."

"It ain't?"

"No," Canyon said, shaking his head, "so you boys obviously have the wrong man. You see, my name isn't Locken."

"Uh-huh," Boyle said. "And you didn't get off the train today wearing western clothes and looking like you just came in off the farm."

"Is that it?" Canyon said. "You don't like farmers? I thought it was something personal."

"Stop fooling around, Boyle," the second man said. "Let's kill him and get out." His hand was on the butt of the .36. Canyon had to make a move before he palmed it.

"All right," Boyle said. "I guess the fun is over." As he said this he spread his hands, so that the gun pointed toward the wall for a split second.

Canyon pulled Locken's sharpened knife out from under the pillow and lunged forward, burying it in Boyle's stomach.

Boyle screamed. Canyon grabbed the gun from his hand and rolled on the floor a few feet, coming to a stop on his knees. The second man had already pulled a .36 from the holster and was pointing it at Canyon. They pulled their respective triggers at the same time.

A .36 slug punched its way into Canyon's left shoulder as his blast took the second man in the belly, throwing him back against the wall.

Canyon stood up and checked both men to make sure they were dead. Then and only then did he stand up and check his own wound. He counted himself lucky that he hadn't purchased a larger-caliber gun from Billy Rosewood.

The police officer in charge introduced himself as Inspector Maxwell of the New York City Police Department. He was standing, staring down at Canyon, who was sitting on the bed with a wadded-up pillowcase pressed against his wound. Actually there were two wounds, an entry and an exit, but neither was serious, as the bullet had simply passed through about an inch of flesh. It was messy and painful, but not serious.

"From the looks of this room," Maxwell said, "you're going to be looking for a new one."

"No," Canyon said, "I just got this one looking the way I want it."

Maxwell looked at the wall next to them, which was covered with the blood of the man who was lying at the base of it.

"Do you know who these two are?" he asked Canyon.

"No," Canyon said. "I don't. They said they followed me from the station. I guess they wanted to rob me."

"That's your guess, is it?"

"Have you got a better one?" Canyon asked. He stared up at the policeman and said, "Do *you* know them?"

"Oh, yes," Maxwell said, "yes, yes, yes, I know them quite well. That is, I *did* know them. For a dollar and a half—each—they'd kill their own mothers. In fact, I think Boyle did just that."

At that moment Boyle's body was being carried from the room by three men, who were having some difficulty.

"Boyle's the big one," Canyon said.

"Right," Maxwell said. "The other one was Clyde something. I can't remember right now."

"And they didn't want to rob me?"

"That's just it," Maxwell said. "Robbery is not their area. They're strongarmers. They break bones for a living, but they didn't rob."

"Then they wanted to break my bones?"

"Didn't they tell you what they wanted?"

"I didn't give them much of a chance," Canyon said. "I assumed they were here to kill me, and I acted as soon as I could to protect myself."

"And killed both of them."

"I guess I got lucky."

"Look, Mr. O'Grady, just what did they say to you?"

"That they had followed me from the station."

"What for?"

"To kill me," Canyon said. "That was what I assumed."

"But they didn't say that to you."

"No."

"Why do you think they wanted to kill you?"

"I don't know."

"What *did* they say to you?"

"That they followed me from the station."

"They say why?"

"No," Canyon said patiently, "they didn't." He saw no reason to mention Locken to the policeman at the moment. He didn't want to get the local law involved until he heard from Wheeler.

"I just assumed that they would have killed me if I didn't do something first."

"Are we back to that again?"

"I'm afraid so."

"And you don't know why?"

"No."

"Have you ever seen them before?"

"Before today?"

"Yes."

"No."

36

"You didn't see them at the train station?"

"I'm afraid not."

"Or spot them following you?"

"I had no reason to think that anyone was following me, Inspector."

"What do you do for a living, Mr. O'Grady?"

The agent was prepared for that question.

"I gamble."

"I see," Maxwell said. His look was disapproving. "Do you think this might be connected with a gambling debt of some sort?"

"It couldn't be."

"Why not?"

"I don't owe anyone any money."

"What about someone who owes you money and might not want to pay?"

"I collect all my debts, Inspector. I don't carry them."

Maxwell still looked as if he thought that a man who could kill both Boyle and Clyde should have been able to spot them following him from the train station. Canyon felt the same way, but did not confide this to the Inspector.

"I suppose you'd like to go to the hospital and have that wound taken care of?" Maxwell asked him.

"I'd like that very much, Inspector."

5

The police transported Canyon O'Grady to a hospital on Second Avenue. The place was a flurry of activity. Canyon saw wounded or dazed people all over the place, and doctors and nurses were rushing about, if they weren't in the act of treating someone.

"My God," Canyon said.

"They don't have emergency rooms where you come from?" Maxwell asked.

"Not like this."

"Come on," Maxwell said, "let's get you treated."

"You really don't have to waste time waiting for me, Inspector."

"Nonsense," Maxwell said. "You're a guest in our city. I want to make sure you're treated properly. Besides, we still have lots to talk about."

"We do?"

"Yes," Maxwell said, "lots." He turned to a uniformed policeman who had accompanied them into the hospital and said, "Get a doctor."

"Yes, sir."

"And find out what's happening here."

"Yes, sir."

Canyon and Maxwell had to move aside as a bleeding

man was carried past them by two orderlies in white uniforms. At least, they had been white until the wounded man bled all over them.

The policeman returned with a frowning doctor, also wearing white.

"What do we have here?" he demanded.

"A bullet wound."

"Serious?" the doctor asked, looking not at Maxwell but at Canyon.

"Not too bad," Canyon said. "It went in and out."

"I can have a nurse dress it," the doctor said, then looked at Maxwell and added, "if that's all right with you?"

"That'll be fine, Doctor," Canyon said. "I can see that you're pretty busy here."

Maxwell looked at the policeman, who said, "A fight on Broadway, sir."

"A fight," the doctor said. "More like a massacre. Nurse!"

A woman stopped, looked around, and then came over. She was a heavyset woman in her forties.

"I need a dressing here, and probably some stitching. Can you take care of that?"

"Uh, well, Doctor—" the woman said, obviously not prepared, for one reason or another, to say yes.

"Then take him someplace out of the way and find someone who can do it."

"Yes, Doctor."

The doctor hurried away and the nurse looked at Canyon and said, "Come with me."

She led him to a small cubicle with a table and chair

and said, "Sit up on the table and wait." She turned and saw Maxwell behind her. "You wait outside."

"I'll be right outside," Maxwell said to Canyon, who simply nodded.

He waited about five minutes before another nurse came in. This one was younger than the first, and beautiful. So beautiful, in fact, that Canyon caught his breath. She had brown eyes with somewhat heavy eyebrows, and a full, lush mouth that looked almost like a smudge. She was about twenty-four, tall and slender, but with bold, solid breasts. At the moment her beautiful face looked a little sad, as if she had seen a lot of pain that night.

"Let me see that," she said. They had draped his jacket over Canyon's shoulders, and beneath it he was still holding a pillowcase to the wound. She removed the case gently, as it was sticking to him somewhat, and when she finally had it free she tossed it aside and studied the wound critically.

"That's not too bad," she said, gracing him with a smile.

He could smell her hair as she leaned close to him, and she must have been on duty for some time, because he could also smell her perspiration, which was not unpleasant.

She cleaned, treated, and dressed the wound quickly and competently, and then stepped back to admire her handiwork.

"Not too bad, even if I do say so myself."

"It's fine," Canyon said. "Thank you. You have gentle hands."

"Have I? Why, thank you."

"Gentle and lovely."

She gave him a stern but amused look and said, "Are you quick with a compliment, Mr. . . . ?"

"O'Grady," he said, "Canyon O'Grady. My friends call me Canyon."

"I see."

"And to answer your question," he went on, "I give compliments when they're deserved."

"Well then, I will accept it in the same spirit it was given."

"And what's your name?"

"I'm Alison Gordon, Mr. O'Grady."

"Canyon, remember?"

"Canyon," she said. "If I were you, Canyon, I would take it easy for the next few days, perhaps even a week. That's not a serious wound, but it could easily start bleeding again."

"I'll be very careful," he said. "I promise."

"Let me help you with your jacket."

"You haven't even asked me how this happened," he said to her.

She laughed softly and said, "Canyon, if I asked everyone who came in here how they got hurt, I'd be here all night listening to tall tales."

"Oh, I have no tall tale to tell," he said, "but I *could* tell it to you over dinner."

Having draped his jacket over his shoulders again, she stepped back to regard him critically.

"Are you asking me to have dinner with you?"

"I thought I did, yes."

"It's quite late," she said, "and I still have an hour to go on my shift."

"I could wait."

"You should go home and rest."

"I'm a long way from home," he said.

"Where are you from?"

"I could tell you that over dinner, too."

She shook her head and said, "You're persistent."

"What's your answer?"

"I suppose if you're around when I get off," she said, "I'll have to decide then."

He smiled at her and said, "Fair enough."

"And now I do have other patients waiting for me. Good night, Canyon."

"Until later," he said.

Alison left, and Maxwell appeared just seconds later.

"All patched up?"

"Yes," Canyon said, standing up. He experienced a moment of dizziness, but it quickly passed.

"Let's go, then," Maxwell said. "We'll take you back to your hotel."

"I think I'd prefer to walk, Inspector," Canyon said. "That is . . . we are within walking distance from my hotel, aren't we?"

"I suppose," Maxwell said, "but do you think you should—"

"Are you concerned, Inspector?"

"Come on," the policeman said, "I'll walk you outside."

The uniformed policeman was waiting for them outside the hospital. The Inspector ignored him and lit a cigarette. He offered Canyon one and he refused it, although had it been a cigar he might not have.

"What else is there, O'Grady?"

"About what?"

"About this," Maxwell said. "I hope you don't expect me to believe that you were just an innocent victim tonight."

"Why not?"

"Because an innocent victim could not have handled the situation the way you did tonight."

"I don't see why not."

Maxwell frowned.

"How long do you intend to remain in New York?"

"Well," Canyon said, "right now, at least until I heal."

"Has it occurred to you that if you stay," Maxwell said, "you might not get the chance to heal?"

"Yes, Inspector, that had occurred to me."

"Then you admit that these two might have been sent after you?"

"It's possible, I suppose."

"Which means there might be more."

Canyon shrugged.

"I'd be very careful if I was you, O'Grady."

"You're the second person to tell me that tonight, Inspector," Canyon said, "and I appreciate it."

"We'll see each other again."

"I hope so," Canyon said. "You still have my guns."

"That's right," Maxwell said, "and I'll bet you'll be needing them again . . . soon."

"What about my knife?"

"Oh," Maxwell said, "I have that here." He took it from his pocket. "I had it cleaned for you inside."

"Much obliged," Canyon said, accepting the knife.

"Your rifle is still in your room, O'Grady," Maxwell said. "Your guns will most likely be returned tomorrow."

"I'll look forward to it."

"If you think of something I should know," the Inspector said, "you will notify me, won't you?"

"Of course, Inspector," Canyon said. "I want to get to the bottom of this just as much as you do."

"I would think you'd like to get to the bottom of this even more than I would, O'Grady," the policeman said, "much more."

"Hello."

The voice jerked Canyon O'Grady from reverie. He had been leaning against the side of the hospital building, thinking about Locken, the Duke, and the two men who had tried to kill him tonight. Even as he turned to face Alison Gordon he was thinking how ludicrous it was for him to be out here waiting for her when the Duke was somewhere in the city—and he *was* in New York. At the very least that was what the night's events told him, for sure.

He looked at Alison, who was looking at him with some amusement, tinged with concern.

"You should really be in bed," she said, and then reddened. He liked her for the blush, but decided not to comment and embarrass her further.

"I thought you might be hungry," he said to her.

"I do usually eat something after work."

"I'm a little hungry myself," he said. "Getting shot sometimes does that to me."

"Oh? Have you been shot a lot?"

"Not a lot," he said. "As a token of my appreciation, I'll buy."

She smiled and said, "Come on. There aren't many restaurants open at this hour, but I know a place."

"Now that I'm not on duty," Alison said later, "I can afford to indulge my curiosity."

"You mean, why was I shot?" he asked.

"Yes."

They were in a small restaurant where Alison usually took her after-work meals. She had been greeted warmly by one of the two waitresses, a woman about her own age. The service was good, and the food was even better. Canyon—with the food and the company—almost didn't mind the throbbing of his wound.

"Well, if you have questions," he said, "ask away."

"First, who shot you?"

"A big, ugly fella named Boyle."

"Why?"

"He didn't say."

"You don't know why you were shot?"

"No."

"That must be very frustrating for you."

She was right, perhaps for the wrong reason, in saying that he felt frustrated.

"What about the other times?" she asked.

"What other times?"

"The other times you were shot. You said there were a lot."

"No," he said, "I said that there weren't a lot."

"Are you in the kind of business where people shoot at you?"

"Only if they lose," he said, deciding to stick with the gambler story.

"Oh? You're a gambler."

"Is it bad if I say yes?"

"I'm not here to pass judgment on you," she said. "If you're good at it, I guess you might as well make a living at it."

"I do all right."

"You're from out West, aren't you?"

"Does it show?"

"Actually, no," she said. "You're not at all what I would have expected from a westerner. Is it as violent out there as we here in the East hear?"

"Only if you go looking for it."

"And you don't?"

"Not if I can help it," he said. "Sometimes—like tonight—it just manages to find me."

He sat back, and the motion made him grimace with pain.

"Does the wound hurt?"

"Yes."

"Maybe it's time you went back to your hotel and got some rest?"

He smiled and said, "Maybe you're right."

He paid the bill and they went outside.

"We didn't get a chance to talk about you," he complained.

"We can do that," she promised with a smile, "another time."

"Well, at least that means there will be another time," he said.

She smiled again and said, "You know where to find me." She pointed and said, "Your hotel is that way. Good night, Canyon O'Grady."

"Good night, Alison."

He watched her walk away until she turned a corner out of sight, then turned and started walking toward his hotel. The street was empty this late at night, and he felt naked without his gun. He also felt like a fool. He was exposed out here because he'd wanted to spend time with a woman he had just met. Still, most of the times in his life he'd been a fool, it had involved a woman.

He kept one hand in his pocket, holding Locken's knife.

6

Canyon woke the next morning to an insistent knock on his door. He staggered from the bed, stopped short when the pain struck him, and then continued to the door more gingerly.

"Your guns," Inspector Maxwell said.

"Thanks," Canyon said, accepting them. "Is that all?"

"Not quite."

"I didn't think so. More conversation?"

"Yes. Can I come in?"

"Can we do this over breakfast?" Canyon asked. In spite of his late meal with Alison, he was hungry.

"Who's buying?"

"I guess I am."

"I'll meet you downstairs."

Canyon got dressed, deliberating about the guns. He couldn't wear the shoulder harness because it would chafe his wound. He decided to take the smaller gun, the .36, and dropped it into his jacket pocket. It dragged the jacket down, but that couldn't be helped. He put the knife in the other pocket, which did little to balance him.

When he got downstairs he found Inspector Maxwell out front, talking to Billy Rosewood.

"You two know each other?" Canyon asked.

"Very well," Maxwell said. "How do you two know each other?"

"Billy gave me a ride from the station."

Maxwell looked at Billy and said, "You wouldn't be selling guns again, would you, Billy? I've warned you about that before."

Before Rosewood could answer Canyon said, "He just gave me a ride."

"Sure," Maxwell said.

"Are we going to have that breakfast?" Canyon asked.

"Not in this hotel dining room," Maxwell said. "I've got too much respect for my stomach."

"I know a place," Canyon said. "A friend showed it to be last night."

"You've got friends in town already?" Maxwell asked.

"Billy's my friend," Canyon said.

"Then you should be more careful how you choose friends."

"Hey!" Rosewood said.

"What are you doing here this morning anyway, Billy?" Maxwell asked.

"He's meeting me," Canyon said, once again rescuing the younger man. "I need someone to show me around."

"Well, Billy's good for that," Maxwell said. "He knows all the real interesting spots."

"The Inspector and I are going to have breakfast, Billy," Canyon said. "Can you meet me back here in an hour?"

"I'll be here," Rosewood said.

"Come on," Canyon said to Maxwell, "we can walk to the restaurant."

"You feel up to it?" Maxwell asked.

"I insist on it," Canyon said.

When they got to the restaurant, Maxwell looked around in frank disapproval. "Who showed you this place?" he asked. Canyon noticed for the first time that the policeman's clothes were a lot more expensive than his.

"I told you," Canyon said, "a friend—a lady friend."

"You've been in town one day," Maxwell said, "and already you've got Billy Rosewood for a friend, *and* you've made the acquaintance of a lady?"

"Let's get a table," Canyon said.

"That shouldn't be too difficult."

The same waitress who had served Canyon and Alison came over and smiled at him.

"Hello. You're Alison's friend."

"That's right."

"The eggs must have been good last night."

"Are they still good?"

"The best."

"We'll have some."

"This way."

Maxwell gave his chair a good close scrutiny before sitting in it.

"I assume you're used to better places than this," Canyon said.

"I usually frequent, uh, cleaner establishments, yes."

"Wait until you taste the eggs," Canyon said. "You might find cleaner, but you won't find better."

"Coffee?" the waitress asked.

"Yes," Canyon said. "Two cups."

"One clean one," Maxwell added.

The waitress gave him a hurt look and went to fill the order.

"You're a mean man," Canyon said. "You hurt her feelings."

"She'll live."

"You have some questions for me?"

"Did you remember anything else from last night?"

"Not a thing."

"Boyle had six hundred dollars on him."

"What about the other man?"

"Boyle carried all the money for both of them."

"Oh," Canyon said, "for a minute there I was almost flattered."

"Anyway," Maxwell said, "it looks like they were paid to kill you."

"That's nice," Canyon said.

The waitress brought the coffee and the eggs. She slammed a cup down in front of Maxwell and said, "Here's the clean one!"

After she left Maxwell said, "Who wants to kill you that bad?"

"I just got to town, Inspector," Canyon said. "I don't know anybody."

"Well, somebody knows you. Somebody had them at the station waiting for you."

Canyon decided it was time for him to give the Inspector something to occupy his time.

"Wait a minute."

"You remember something?" Maxwell asked. He was eating the eggs without a hint of dissatisfaction.

"Yeah, the big one, Boyle . . . he called me Locken."

"Locken?"

"Yep."

"Well, I guess they thought you were this Locken guy," Maxwell said around his eggs.

"I guess so. Maybe you can find out if a man named Locken came into town on the same train I did."

"I'll check on it after breakfast."

"How are the eggs?"

Maxwell stopped short as he was shoveling the last of his eggs into his mouth and said, "Uh, they're not bad."

"Here," Canyon said, dropping some money on the table, "eat mine."

"Where are you going?"

"I'm going to church," Canyon said, and left.

He found Billy Rosewood still waiting for him in front of his hotel.

"Are you in trouble with the police, Mr. O'Grady?" the young man asked.

"Are you?"

Rosewood smiled sheepishly.

"The Inspector and I are acquainted, but they can't

arrest me for anything. What happened to you last night? You're standin' funny."

"I got shot last night."

"How?"

"With that gun you got me."

Rosewood looked alarmed.

"Hey, it ain't my fault if you shot yourself. I thought you knew how to handle a gun—"

"I didn't shoot myself, Billy," Canyon said. "I had a couple of visitors."

"What? Who?"

"I'll tell you later. I have to go inside and check with the desk for a minute. I'll be right back. Stay out of trouble."

"Always!"

Canyon went inside to the front desk.

"Are there any messages for me?" he asked the officious-looking desk clerk.

"Your name?"

"O'Grady."

"Oh, yes . . ." the clerk said, looking frustrated, "Mr. O'Grady. Ah, if you would like another room—"

"The one I have is just fine," Canyon said. "All I need are my messages."

"Yes, sir, of course," the man said. He had the kind of mustache Canyon thought was ridiculous. It was pencil-thin and hardly visible. The man turned, took something from the big agent's message box, and handed it to him. It was a telegraph flimsy.

"Thank you."

"Are you sure you wouldn't like another room, sir?" the clerk said. "We like our guests to be satisfied—"

"I'm very satisfied, thank you," Canyon assured him, and went back outside.

"Where are we headed?" Rosewood asked.

"Just get going and I'll let you know," Canyon told him, climbing into the cab.

Inside the cab he read the message. It said:

O'GRADY:
SEE THE POSTMAN. 483 BROOME STREET.
REGARDS FROM RUFUS.

"Do you know where Broome Street is," Canyon shouted up to Rosewood.

"Sure I do."

"Take me to four eighty-three."

Getting there was the easy part, but once he got there who the hell was he supposed to see—and what was this business about a postman?

7

The chipped and faded writing on the door still said clearly enough WALTER POSTMAN, and the address was 483 Broome Street. That answered both of Canyon O'Grady's questions.

The man who addressed his knock was big, well over six feet tall, and wider than the doorway. He had a black, grease-covered beard that extended down to his chest, and he was still chewing. The suit he was wearing could only be called ill-fitting, but as with Inspector Maxwell, it had obviously cost more than the one Canyon was wearing.

The odd thing about the man was his eyes. They were blue and almost gentle-looking. They were probably a great disadvantage in his business . . . whatever his business was.

"Yeah, what?" His voice fit his eyes rather than his appearance. Another disadvantage.

"Mr. Postman?"

"That's right."

"I bring greetings from a friend."

"Oh, yeah? Who?"

"Rufus Wheeler."

"Wheeler," Postman said, nodding. He chewed the

last of the food in his mouth and asked, "Who are you?"

"O'Grady."

"Oh, yeah . . ." Postman said, looking him up and down. "So you're O'Grady."

"I'm O'Grady."

"I heard of you."

"I never heard of you."

"That's the first good news I've had all week," Postman said. "Come on in and shut the door behind you."

Postman backed away and Canyon entered, closing the door as instructed.

Postman went around behind his desk and sat down. On the desk in front of him was a plate of bacon and eggs, and another with biscuits and butter. There was also a pot of coffee. From the way the room smelled Canyon might have thought Postman had cooked the food himself.

"Want some?" Postman asked.

"No, thanks."

"I got a stove in the other room. It's no trouble."

"That's okay," Canyon said. "I had breakfast."

"Coffee?"

"Sure."

Postman took a cup out of the bottom drawer and handed it to Canyon, who blew some dust out of it before pouring himself coffee. Then he sat in a straight-backed chair in front of Postman's desk.

"What can I do for you, then?" Postman asked.

"That's what I was going to ask you," Canyon said.

He handed the man the telegraph message from Wheeler. Postman read it and grunted. Canyon would find out that the man had a grunt for any occasion.

"You don't mind if I finish eating while we talk, do you?" Postman asked.

"No, go right ahead," Canyon said. He quickly outlined his desires.

Postman wiped his hand on his jacket. "So you're lookin' for the Duke, huh?"

"You know him?" Canyon asked.

"I've heard of him, yeah." Postman picked up a biscuit and buttered it.

"I think he's in New York," Canyon said.

"What makes you think that?"

"Information from a friend."

"A friend named Locken?"

"That's right."

"Locken dead?"

"Yes."

"They gun him?"

"In the back."

Postman made a face.

"I knew Locken," he said.

"I did too," Canyon said, "a long time. I want the man who had him killed."

"The Duke."

"That's right."

"All right," Postman said, "here's what I know. It came to me over a secure line from Washington. 'Duke' is a sort of code name for some fella who has something to sell."

"Like what?"

"Information about the people you work for."

"You work for them too, don't you?"

"Sometimes."

"What kind of information are we talking about?"

"I don't know all the particulars," Postman said. "Damagin' information. It was Locken's job to stop this fella. I guess it's your job now."

"It's more than a job to me, but I know what you mean," Canyon said. "I don't know this town, Postman. I need help."

"Where are you staying?"

"A hotel on Twenty-third street—the St. Martin's Hotel."

Postman was nodding to himself, chewing on a piece of biscuit.

"All right, O'Grady. I'll see what I can find out."

Canyon stood up. "Thanks."

"Don't forget your paper."

Canyon reached over and picked it up. He started for the door and was stopped by Postman's voice.

"Hey, O'Grady."

"Yeah?"

"Did he try for you yet?"

"Yeah, at my hotel. Two of them."

"They both dead?"

"Yep."

"They know who you were?"

"They thought I was Locken."

"So nobody knows who you really are?"

"No."

"Not even the police?"

"They know my name, but that's all. I told them I was a gambler."

"Who from the police was in charge?"

"Inspector Maxwell?"

Postman nodded.

"I know him."

Canyon wanted, but Postman did not comment further on Maxwell.

"Go back to your hotel," Postman said. "I'll get in touch with you there."

"Leave a message if I'm out."

"Don't *be* out."

"I didn't come all this way to sit in a hotel room, Postman," Canyon said.

Postman frowned and then said, "I'll catch up with you."

"I appreciate your help," Canyon said. "I'll leave and let you finish your . . . breakfast."

Outside, Rosewood said to him, "Where are we going now?"

Canyon looked at him and asked, "Do you know any good churches?"

"What kind of churches?"

"The kind that serve liquor, of course."

Rosewood took him to a section of the city called Printing House Square. He explained that this was where all of the major New York newspapers were published.

"We're at the east side of City Hall Park and the north end of Park Row. See that statue over there?"

"I see it."

"That's Ben Franklin." Rosewood pointed again and said, "That's the *Herald*." He was pointing to a magnificent marble structure. It was easily the most conspicuous building in the Square. It was located on the corners of Broadway and Anne streets. Later they passed the building that housed the *Tribune*, which was on Nassau and Spruce streets.

When they were in a saloon, sitting at a table with a couple of cold beers, Rosewood said, "Listen."

"To what?"

"Just to the conversations that are going on."

Canyon listened for several minutes, eavesdropping on three or four different conversations, and they each centered on the same thing.

"Money," Billy Rosewood said. "That's why every once in a while I come down here, park, and tour the saloons. I can smell the money in the air."

Canyon had wondered why Rosewood, dressed as inexpensively as he was, had not drawn any curious glances when they'd entered the saloon. Now he knew.

"They're used to you, aren't they?" he asked.

"Yeah, I've been doing this for a while," Rosewood said. "They objected at first. I even got thrown out of one or two places, but they finally came to accept me, like I was one of the tables or chairs."

"And me?"

He shrugged.

"I guess they accept you because you're with me."

"You ever take anyone else with you?"

"No."

"Why me?"

Rosewood shrugged again.

"Guess I never liked anyone well enough."

"I'm flattered."

"Would you like to tell me about last night?"

Canyon thought a moment, then decided to go ahead and tell him about Boyle and Clyde. In fact, he told him everything he'd told Inspector Maxwell. He did not, however, tell Rosewood what he had told Postman.

"And you don't know why they wanted to kill you?"

"I have to assume that they just mistook me for someone else."

"So, what *are* you doing in New York?"

Canyon shrugged.

"I've never been here before. I thought it was time."

"Uh-huh, you're just on vacation."

"That's right."

"And I suppose you're a peace-loving, churchgoing man who just got lucky last night against two killers."

"I never said that."

"Well, at least you don't think I'm stupid."

"I never said, or thought, that, either." Canyon checked the time and said, "Any of these places serve decent food?"

"Yeah, as a matter of fact, this one serves real good steak and onion sandwiches."

"All right," Canyon said, "I'll buy you lunch."

"I thought you might," Rosewood said, smiling, "so

when I went to the bar for the beers, I ordered for both of us.''

"See?" Canyon said to the younger man. "Definitely not stupid.''

8

It was late afternoon when Rosewood dropped Canyon off at his hotel.

"Will you need me later?"

Canyon thought a moment, then smiled and asked, "Would you be available at two in the morning?"

"If that's when you want me."

"You know the hospital I was at?"

Rosewood gave him an exasperated look and asked, "Don't you know by now that I know where everything in this city is?"

"Okay," Canyon said, "stupid question. Go to that hospital at two A.M. and pick up a nurse."

"You got one nurse in mind?"

Canyon smiled and described Alison Gordon in detail. Billy Rosewood was impressed.

"After you've picked her up, take her to—what's a decent restaurant open at that time of night?"

"There ain't many," Rosewood said, "but lucky for you I happen to know of one." He described a place quickly.

"Good. Bring her there, and have someone pick me up and bring me there."

"I know just the fella. His name is Archie."

"Is he expensive?"

"You pay me," Rosewood said, "not him."

"Okay, deal."

"I'll take care of everything, Mr. O'Grady," Rosewood said. "Don't worry about a thing."

"The name's Canyon, Billy, and I'm not worried."

Canyon waved and went into the hotel lobby. As he entered he saw the clerk behind the desk nod to someone. A man seated in the lobby stood up and approached Canyon, who slipped his hand into his pocket and closed it around the .36.

"O'Grady?"

"That's right."

"The Postman sent me."

The man was tall and thin, well dressed, but not as expensively as Postman. He didn't appear to be armed, but that might have been due to the cut of his suit.

"You got something for me?"

"A message," the man said. "You want it here?"

"No," Canyon said, "let's go up to my room. After you."

The man hesitated, then moved ahead of Canyon.

When they reached the door to his room, Canyon removed the .36 from his pocket and pressed it to the small of the man's back.

"What's goin' on?" the man asked.

"I'm just being careful, friend," Canyon said. "Don't take offense. Raise your hands, please."

The man did as he was told and Canyon searched him. He found a .38 caliber Colt under his arm and nothing else. He returned his own gun to his pocket and held the man's .38.

"All right, let's go inside."

Canyon opened the door and the man preceded him into the room.

"Not bad," the man said, looking around.

"What's your name?" Canyon asked.

"Largo, Jim Largo."

"Sit on the bed, Mr. Largo."

Largo did as he was told.

"What's this message you have for me?"

"The Postman sent me because he thought you might be needing some help."

"Why would he think that?"

Largo looked around the room, at the blood on the floor and the wall which had not quite been scrubbed out, and said, "I guess he just has a feeling."

"You tell your Postman that I'll be fine," Canyon said. "I don't need a bodyguard."

Largo stood up, "I'll tell him."

"Make sure you also tell him that I appreciate the offer."

"My gun, please?" Largo said.

Canyon hesitated for a moment, then handed the gun over. The man slid it back into his shoulder rig.

"Postman hasn't located my man yet." It was more a statement than a question.

"No."

"Something occurs to me, Mr. Largo."

"What's that?"

"This man I'm looking for . . . "

"The Duke?" Largo asked. The look on his face gave away what he thought of anyone who would use such a name.

"That's right," Canyon said, "the Duke. What would he do when he got to town?"

"I don't know," Largo said. "What?"

"Probably the same thing I did. He'd look for help."

"You sayin' that this Duke fella went to Postman for help?"

"Not Postman," Canyon said, "but maybe somebody like him."

Largo grinned.

"There isn't anyone else like the Postman."

"But I'll bet there are men who try to make their living the same way."

"I suppose."

"Ask the Postman to look around at some of the other . . . suppliers in the city."

"Postman knows what he's doing, O'Grady."

"Just tell him," Canyon said. "It can't hurt."

"I'll tell him," Largo said, "but he won't appreciate the suggestion."

Canyon had nothing to say to that. Largo walked to the door, opened it, and then turned to face Canyon.

"I don't take kindly to having my gun taken away from me," he said.

Canyon grinned tightly and said, "Next time you come to see me, don't wear it."

* * *

66

At 1:45 A.M. Canyon left the hotel and found a horse-drawn cab waiting for him outside, a young man leaning against it. His name was Archie, and he told Canyon to climb aboard.

After a while O'Grady saw a street sign that said East Forty-third Street, and recalled that was the street Rosewood had said the restaurant was on. Moments later they pulled up in front of the place.

He stepped out of the cab and saw that this was a far cry from the little restaurant where he and Alison had shared a meal.

"This place is gonna cost you plenty," Archie said with a smirk. "I hope the girl is worth it."

"She is."

Archie looked up and down the deserted street and said, "I hope she shows up."

"So do I," Canyon said. "I'll be inside, Archie."

"Okay, boss."

Canyon entered the restaurant and was met at the door by a man in a tuxedo.

"Sir?"

"O'Grady."

"Yes, sir. This way, please."

Canyon followed the man to a table, where the man held his chair for him.

"Your waiter will be here shortly."

"No hurry," Canyon said, "I'm waiting for a young lady."

"Ah," the man said with no expression, and left Canyon to his own devices.

Canyon admired the interior, which was all crystal

and leather. As deserted as it was outside, inside it was very busy. There were no empty tables as far as he could see.

There was a clock on the wall by which he could see it was ten minutes past two. He was beginning to worry that Billy Rosewood might not have been persuasive enough when Alison Gordon suddenly came into view, following the man in the tuxedo. She was wearing her nurse's uniform and a stern look.

"Your companion, sir," the man said, holding her chair for her.

"Thank you," she said.

"I will send your waiter over."

Canyon nodded, and the man left them.

"I will never forgive you for this," Alison said to Canyon.

"For what, exactly?" he asked. "I hope Billy wasn't too—"

"Not for Billy," she said. "For this . . . this place."

"What's wrong with it?"

"Nothing. It's one of the most expensive restaurants in New York, which is why they stay open so late, in order to accommodate all of their patrons."

"Then why are you so—" he started, but she cut him off, leaning over and speaking in an urgent whisper.

"This is the most expensive restaurant in the city!" she said.

"That's all right, I can afford it."

"That's not it."

"Then wha—"

"You had me brought here dressed like this!" she said. "I look like . . . like . . ."

"Alison," Canyon said, "take my word for it, you are the most beautiful woman in the place."

She stared at him and said, "My God, you're impossible."

Postman looked up from the stack that was spread out over most of his desk as Jim Largo walked into his office. He saw a familiar look on Largo's face. The look usually meant that his right-hand man had found someone he thought was interesting—and "interesting" to Largo meant a worthy opponent.

"Did you see him?" Postman asked.

"I did."

Postman took a drink from a pail of beer he'd had brought up to him from a nearby saloon. Some of the beer slopped over onto his beard and chest. Largo was used to his boss's sloppy eating habits, and they no longer disgusted him.

"You've got that look on your face, James," Postman said. "What is it?"

"He took my gun away from me."

"Really?" Postman said. "How surprising. I wouldn't have thought you'd let that happen."

"He's interesting."

"Uh-huh," Postman said. "He's not for you, James. Find some other way to prove your manhood."

Largo ignored his boss's jibe.

"He had a suggestion for you."

"And what's that?"

Largo told Postman about Canyon's idea, and the fat man sat back and pondered it.

"I dislike being told what to do . . ." he said.

"I told him you would."

" . . . but the idea does have merit. Follow up on it. Check with Taylor, Sadler . . . and Liston. See if they know anything."

"All right," Largo said, turning to leave. "I'd bet on Taylor."

"And, Largo?"

"Yes?"

"Try to control that competitive streak of yours where this one is concerned. He's a friend of a friend."

Largo looked at Postman and said, "A friend of a friend of yours, not mine."

After dinner, Billy Rosewood drove Canyon and Alison back to his hotel, but they did not get out.

"Do you want me to come up?" she asked.

"Maybe another time."

"What?" she asked. "You're a strange man, Canyon O'Grady, and I'll bet not a shy one."

"I'm not shy," he said. "I want you to come up, but it might not be safe."

"Well," she said, smiling, "your wound is much too fresh for any kind of . . . strenuous activity."

"What kind of activity did you have in mind?" he asked. "Maybe we can—"

"Never mind," she said. "Get out of the cab so your friend can drive me home."

"Maybe we could dine together again soon," he said.

"Perhaps."

He climbed out of the cab, then turned to bid her good-night.

"Tomorrow is my day off," she said suddenly.

"Did you have something in mind?"

She cocked her head to one side and asked, "Have you ever seen a baseball game?"

Canyon frowned and was about to say something when she said quickly, "Never mind. Pick me up at eleven A.M. We'll see a game and have a picnic lunch."

"All right," he said. "I'm game."

"I hope so," she said. "Good night."

9

When Canyon came out of his hotel the following morning, Billy Rosewood was waiting out front.

"Didn't do so good last night, did you?" Rosewood asked.

"And what makes you say that?"

"Well, the lady went home kind of early, didn't she?"

"That's because we have a date today," Canyon said.

"Oh? To do what?"

"To see a baseball game."

"How romantic. That won't be until later. You want breakfast?"

"Sure."

"Come on," Rosewood said. "I know a place."

Rosewood took Canyon to a restaurant on Roosevelt Street. When the waiter came they ordered breakfast and Rosewood explained what little he knew about baseball.

"I'm not a fan or anything," he said, "and I've never been to a game, but as I understand it the object of the game is to hit a ball that is thrown by a man, uh, with a stick that they call a bat."

"And what do you do after you hit it?"

"Uh . . . run."

"To where?"

Rosewood frowned and said, "You'd better wait until you and the lady go to the game, O'Grady. She'll be able to explain it to you better."

"I'm sure she will," Canyon said. "She couldn't do it any worse."

After they'd finished breakfast, Rosewood took him to Alison Gordon's residence. He knew the way because he'd taken her there the night before.

"It's in Five Points, on Mulberry Street," Rosewood said. "Bad part of town."

"What's she doing there?"

"The obvious reason would be because she can't afford to live anyplace else."

"She has a good job."

Rosewood shrugged and said, "She must have been born there."

He stopped in front of Alison's building and Canyon got out.

"Second floor rear," Rosewood called down from his perch.

"Got it."

Canyon entered the building and climbed the rickety stairs to the second floor. Apparently there were two apartments on each floor, and he walked to the rear and knocked on the door.

"Hello," Alison said as she opened the door.

"Hi."

They stood there for a few seconds and then he said, "Can I come in?"

"Oh, I'm sorry," she said, stepping back. "Of course, come in."

He entered and she closed the door. The place was modestly furnished, but it was very clean and well kept.

"Not much, I know," she said.

"I've seen worse."

"Have you?" she asked. "Where?"

"All over the West," he said. "In fact, in some places this would be thought of as luxurious."

"I haven't been anywhere but here," she said. "I'd love to travel." She looked at Canyon and said, "When you're born in Five Points, all you can do it hope to travel, to get out, one day."

"You have a good job," he said, echoing what he'd said to Rosewood. "Surely you can save some money."

"I am trying," she said. "Shall we go? The game starts at noon."

"I'm afraid you'll have to explain this game to me," he said as they walked to the door. "In detail."

"Oh, I will," she said. "I just love watching them play. I'm sure you will like it too."

"I'm sure I will," Canyon said, but without conviction.

As it turned out he did enjoy it.

He found himself wondering how the man with the bat could possibly hit the ball, given the speed with which it was being thrown. Also, he wondered why there were times a man could hit the ball so solidly, and yet get nothing for it, and other times he didn't hit the ball at all and was awarded "first base."

"I can't quite understand the rules of this game. It

must take years of practice to play correctly," he said to Alison at one point.

"I'm sure it does," she said.

The New York Knickerbocker Baseball Club was playing St. Louis. Alison explained that they were in something called The National Association of Baseball Players."

"How do you know so much about baseball?" Canyon asked her.

"I used to see one of the players," she said. "I got tired of him, but got very interested in the game."

"I'm glad," he said. She looked at him and he added, "That you're so interested in the game, I mean. You're able to explain it to me so well."

"Of course," she said, and went back to watching.

On the way back to her apartment Canyon said, "We could have a late lunch or an early dinner."

"I have to change."

"Would you like me to come back and pick you up?"

"No," she said. "You can come and wait."

"All right."

Rosewood stopped in front of Alison's building, and Canyon told him to wait.

"How long?"

"Just long enough for the lady to change," Canyon said.

Rosewood gave him a sly look which Canyon ignored.

Upstairs Alison said, "I won't take long."

"That's all right," he said. "I'm sure you'll be well worth waiting for."

"You're sweet," she said. "Five minutes."

While he was waiting Canyon walked to the window and looked down at the back of the building. There was an alley, filled with debris but accessible.

"By the way," he called out, "we didn't decide. Shall we make it late lunch or an early dinner?"

He heard her come out and turned. When he saw her he stopped, stunned. She was indeed well worth waiting for.

She stood in the doorway, naked.

"How about a *late* dinner?" she asked.

"It's Taylor."

Postman looked up from his lunch at Largo.

"As we suspected," he said.

"Yes," Largo said, "as *we* suspected."

"What did you find out?"

"Taylor's put out a call for Razor and Coles."

Postman chewed thoughtfully on a bite of turkey sandwich.

"There's only one thing those boys do well," he said. "Kill."

Postman looked up at Jim Largo and said, "Isn't that your particular talent also, James?"

"It is," Largo said, "but they're not like me."

"They're good."

"Not as good as me," Largo said. "Don't even suggest that."

"All right, my friend, all right," Postman said. "Just keep an eye on O'Grady."

"I don't think that man needs a babysitter," Jim Largo said.

"He's in a strange city," Postman said. "That's a disadvantage to anyone."

"I suppose."

"Just keep an eye on him," Postman said. "You can do that, can't you, James?"

"I can do anything you pay me to do, Postman."

Albert Taylor watched the man who called himself the Duke enter his store. It was at this same time yesterday that the Duke had first made his appearance.

"The sign," Taylor reminded the Duke, who turned and flipped the sign on the door around so that anyone reading it from the outside would see the word "CLOSED."

"Do you have what we discussed for me?" the Duke asked.

"I have two men," Taylor said. "They're good, and they're expensive."

"If they do what they're supposed to do, they'll be worth it."

This fella the Duke was a puzzle to Taylor. Taylor had lived in New York all his life, but he'd known all kinds of tough men. The Duke struck him as the kind of man who might even be a schoolteacher, or anything other than what he was presenting himself as. He wasn't big, and he wasn't mean-looking. Still, there was something about the man that made you pay attention to what he had to say.

"They'll do what they're supposed to do," Taylor said.

"I'll want to meet them before I use them."

"I'll set it up," Taylor said. "Tell me where you're staying."

"No," the Duke said. "I'll meet with them somewhere public."

"Where?"

The Duke shrugged. "This is your city."

"How about a park?"

"Fine."

"All right, then," Taylor said. "Central Park." He gave the Duke directions. "Do you want to see them separately or together?"

"Separately, I think."

"It's better that way," Taylor agreed. "I don't know what would happen if these two came together in the same place. They're both kind of . . . excitable."

"All the better," the Duke said. "What are their names?"

"One is named Armand Coles," Taylor said. "A Frenchman, I think—or at least he wants people to think that. The other is just called Razor."

"Razor."

"Yes."

"Set my meeting with Razor first," the Duke said, "and then with Coles."

"Whatever you say," Taylor answered. "You're the man with the money. I'll, uh, need that down payment we agreed on yesterday."

The Duke took a brown envelope from his pocket and put it down gently on the counter.

"Count it if you want."

"No need," Taylor said. He took the envelope and slipped it underneath the counter. He'd count it as soon as the Duke left, before the man could get too far away.

"The rest will be due when the job is done," Taylor reminded him.

"That's what we agreed on," the Duke said, nodding. He went to the door, flipped the sign back around, and left.

Canyon O'Grady got out of his clothes as quickly and gracefully as he could, and then moved to take Alison Gordon into his arms. Her flesh was like fire and silk at the same time. He kissed her lips, her chin, her shoulders, worked his way to her breasts. He held each breast in his hands, in turn kissing them and biting her nipples. She moaned and grabbed for him, pulling him to her bed. They tumbled onto it together and proceeded to become lost in each other.

He explored her entire body with his mouth, using his mouth and tongue to bring her orgasm after orgasm while she cried out and writhed beneath him.

Later, they exchanged roles. She took him into her mouth and used her mouth and tongue, her teeth and her nails, to tease him to bursting, and then backed off to make him wait longer.

When he finally could absolutely not wait any longer he reached for her, placed her roughly on her back, mounted her, and drove himself into her. She screamed and wrapped her arms and legs around him.

"Oh, God, Canyon, yes . . ." she cried out, raking his back with her nails as he pounded into her. "Ooooh, oh, yes, damn, yes, yes, please . . ."

He cupped her buttocks in his hands, squeezing them so hard that he would leave his fingerprints there. Those would be his marks, just as the scratches on his back would be hers.

And they would leave other marks on each other that night, marks that no one else could see . . . .

Canyon sat up and watched as Alison got dressed.

"Are you going to just look, or get dressed?" she asked him.

He smiled and said, "I'll get dressed after you. I don't want to miss a single move."

"I said it before and I'll say it again," she said. "You're sweet."

There was no longer ever a hint of the awkwardness that had been between them the night before.

Outside Alison Gordon's apartment house, across the street, Jim Largo stood with his arms folded. It hadn't taken him long to find out where Canyon was. Just as the Postman had Largo, so Largo had his own man.

He wouldn't be working for the Postman forever.

10

The Duke was an hour early for the meeting, and he used the time to study that area of the park. It was thick with foliage and trees, but there was a path, with benches along the way. It was quite beautiful, and could probably be quite dangerous after dark.

The Duke was sitting on the bench when a man approached. He was a stocky man, thick through the shoulders and chest and with slightly bandy legged. From where he sat, the Duke could see that the man did not wear a gun.

Then again, his name was Razor.

"You the Duke?" the man asked him.

"I am."

"Is that for real?" the man asked.

"What?"

"That name? The Duke? You ain't a real duke, are you?"

"It's what I'm called," the Duke said coldly.

"Sure," Razor said. "Everybody's got to have a name, right? Taylor said you might have some work for me."

"I might, if you're up to it."

"What's the job?"

"One man."

"I'm up to it."

"Did you know some men named Boyle and Clyde?"

"Second-raters," the man said. He was still standing, shifting his weight from one foot to the other.

"The man I want you to kill killed them."

"That's no recommendation."

"Maybe not," the Duke said. "Taylor says you're one of the best."

"He's wrong," Razor said. "I am the best. Who's the man and where do I find him?"

"His name's O'Grady . . ." the Duke said, and told Razor what hotel he was staying at. "Taylor may be able to get you some more information about him."

"It would help if he had a lady," Razor said. He took a straight razor out of his pocket and said, "I like cutting their ladies . . . first."

The Duke looked into the man's eyes and saw madness.

"I don't know if he has a lady," the Duke said, "and I don't care. I just want the man killed."

"Why not kill him yourself?"

The Duke didn't answer.

"Are you afraid of him?" Razor asked. He moved closer to the Duke and waved his razor slowly in his face. "Do you scare easy, friend?"

Faster than Razor would have guessed, the Duke—a smaller man than Razor—grabbed the man's wrist, twisted it, and forced Razor to his knees. He added a little more pressure and the razor fell to the ground. From a folded newspaper on the bench the Duke took a two-shot derringer and pressed it against Razor's temple. The whole display had a practiced but effective look.

"All right, all right," Razor said, gasping at the pain in his wrist, "you can let go now. You proved your point."

"I should kill you," the Duke said, cocking the gun.

"Then you *would* have to kill this O'Grady yourself, wouldn't you?"

The Duke decided not to tell Razor about Armand Coles. He released him and sat back on the bench. Razor retrieved his razor and stood up.

"When do you want this done?"

"As soon as possible."

"Do you care how it looks?"

"I don't care how you do it, as long as he looks dead when you're done."

"All right," Razor said. He put his straight razor away and rubbed his wrist. "All right. You'll know when it's been done. After that, you go and see Taylor and settle up."

"I'll be there."

Razor nodded, turned and left. The Duke checked his watch and saw that he had half an hour before Armand Coles would arrive. He picked up the newspaper on the bench next to him, unfolded it, and started to read.

Razor was a proud man—and a mad one. Mad, and angry. He rubbed his wrist as he walked through the park. He'd kill O'Grady, all right, but after Taylor had collected from the Duke he'd perform his next operation for free—on the Duke!

The Duke! That was a laugh.

As the second man came into view on the path the Duke folded the newspaper and put it down. He made sure the gun was out of sight beneath the folds.

"Are you the man I am to meet?"

The Duke looked up at the man and said, "Are you Coles?"

"I am."

Coles spoke with a French accent. He was taller and slenderer than Razor. If the Duke didn't know better he would have thought that Coles—certainly more graceful than Razor—was the man who killed with a blade.

"I'm the Duke."

Coles sat down on the bench, apparently perfectly relaxed. The folded newspaper with the derringer was on the bench between them. The man made no comment about the name.

"What's the job?"

"I want a man named O'Grady killed," the Duke said. He no longer mistook O'Grady for Locken. The mistake had been remedied, at the cost of two lives. He now assumed that O'Grady had simply replaced Locken on his trail.

He explained that O'Grady had killed Boyle and Clyde—Coles had the same reaction to the news that Razor'd had—and told Coles what hotel O'Grady was in.

"I knew that."

The Duke frowned.

"How?"

"I read the papers," Coles said. "I know what hotel Boyle and Clyde were killed in. The papers didn't say who killed them, however."

"Well, now you know."

The Duke studied Coles. He was obviously more intelligent and less mad than Razor. The Duke decided to tell him more than he had told the first killer.

"I've hired two of you, you know."

"That would make sense. Who's the other?"

"Razor."

Coles made a face.

"What's the matter?"

"He's a barbarian, and he is crazy."

"So I gathered."

"Does he know about me?"

"No. I want you to watch Razor and let him try first. If he fails, then you go in."

"And if he succeeds?"

"Then I'll pay you both."

"And if Razor is killed, and I succeed?"

The Duke smiled. Coles was a man after his own heart.

"Then I'll pay you double."

Coles smiled and nodded.

"What's your weapon?" the Duke asked.

"Oh," Coles said nonchalantly, "anything I find at hand—like this!"

Too late the Duke realized what Coles was doing,

and he was too slow to stop him. In a split second he was looking down the barrel of his own derringer.

"What was this for?" Coles asked.

"I was sure one of you would be crazy," the Duke said.

"And you were right, weren't you?"

"I was right," the Duke said, but looking into Coles' eyes now, he wasn't sure which of the two men was crazier.

Coles took the derringer off cock and handed it back to the Duke. The feverish glint in his eyes was gone as quickly as it had come.

"When do you want it done?" Coles asked.

"I told Razor as soon as possible. Will you know where to find him?"

"I'll find him," Coles said. "If he's too slow I'll kill him, and then O'Grady."

As Coles stood up and Duke said, "I don't care how it works, as long as O'Grady ends up dead."

"Oh, he will," Armand Coles said. "He will."

11

Canyon heard a man's shoe scrape on the windowsill. Alison was deadweight on his arm, and by the time he got his arm out from underneath her it was too late. His recent wound was bleeding, and he was in danger of contracting a new one.

The intruder was on him, and a fist crashed into his face. He fell off the bed, reaching for the gun on the night table, but the man was there before him.

"My God—Canyon!" Alison called out.

"Quiet!" the intruder snapped. "Turn up some light, woman!"

"Canyon?"

"Do as he says."

Alison struck a match and turned up the lamp. In the yellow light she looked golden—and very naked.

Canyon looked up from the floor and saw that the man was eyeing Alison, a hungry look on his face. Before he could react, however, the intruder had Alison by the hair and was holding a straight razor to her throat.

"Easy," Canyon said.

"This one is a real beauty, huh?" the man said.

Canyon didn't reply. He was watching the man carefully, waiting for a chance to move.

"I said she's a beauty, ain't she?" the man said again. He obviously wanted an answer.

"Yes, she is beautiful," Canyon said. "Now, take it easy, friend."

"I ain't your friend!" the man said. He looked at Alison and added, "But I'd like to be hers. Yeah!"

The man moved his hand down from Alison's neck to her breasts and pressed the razor blade against one of her nipples. She gasped but did not try to pull away.

"Real nice!" he said.

"Canyon—" Alison said, biting her lower lip to keep it from quivering.

"Look," Canyon said carefully, "maybe you've got the wrong room here—"

"I've got the right room, the right man, and the right girl," the man told him.

After making love the first time in Alison's room they had gone out to dinner and then returned to the room. Obviously, this madman had followed them back. Canyon thought bitterly that he had done nothing but make mistakes since he had come to New York, and this one might cost Alison her life.

The man with the razor leaned down and spoke into Alison's ear.

"How many men you got, gal?"

"She only has one," Canyon said. "Me."

"Sure," the man said, pressing his blade tightly against her nipple. A small drop of blood appeared, and she gasped again. "That's what they like you to think, friend, that you're the only one."

Canyon frowned. "You don't like women very much, do you?"

"I like them," the man said, "I like them fine . . . I like to cut their nipples off." He looked at Canyon and added, "And I like their men to watch while I do it."

"Only I'm not her man."

The man frowned and said, "You said you was."

"I lied."

"Then who's her man?"

"His name's Locken," Canyon said, "and he's due back here any minute. In fact, I was just getting ready to leave."

"That's okay," the man said. "We've got time. I can cut off her tits, and then kill you both and be out of here real quick." He circled her nipple with the razor and said, "I've done this before, you know. You start here . . . cut around . . . and it comes right off in your hand." He slid his hand beneath one of Alison's breasts to cup and lift it. "I've cut off some big ones. These aren't too big, but they're nice and firm. In fact, they probably weigh as much as a small puppy—each."

"Look," Canyon said, "it's like I told you, I've got to get out of here before her man comes home—and if you're going to cut her, I don't want to see it."

Canyon had gotten to his feet as he spoke and was in a much better position to do something.

The man with the razor was confused.

"What are you doin'?"

"I'm getting dressed."

"No, you're not."

The .36 was in the man's pocket, and he had his razor in one hand and one of Alison's breasts in the other. As if he suddenly realized this, the man realized Alison and groped for his pocket. That was when Canyon moved.

The big agent launched himself over the bed and slammed into the man. They went to the floor together and Canyon felt the man's razor lay open his back. When they landed the man's free hand, the one groping for the gun, was pinned beneath Canyon. The other hand was trying to bring the razor around again. Canyon brought his elbow around and viciously clubbed the man in the face with it. The man grunted, and Canyon grabbed his wrist and slammed the hand down onto the floor. The impact jarred the blade loose, and it skittered across the floor.

Canyon rolled off the man and got to his feet. As the man also tried to get to his feet Canyon hit him in the face again, this time with his fist. The man went over backward, but as he did he finally got the gun free from his pocket. Canyon jumped him, grabbing for the gun with both hands. He closed them around the man's wrist and they struggled for the gun until it went off. Luckily, Canyon had managed to twist the man's hand around, and when the gun fired, the bullet went into the man's belly. Canyon felt the body go taut beneath him, and then limp. He grabbed the gun and staggered back from the body.

He looked around for Alison. She was sitting up on the bed, wide-eyed and trembling.

"Are you all right?" he asked.

"Y-yes," she said, "but your back—"

"What?"

He reached behind him and felt the slick blood covering his back.

"Jesus," he muttered. He was collecting more scars on this adventure . . . .

"Where's the body?" Inspector Maxwell asked as he entered the room.

"What makes you think there's a body?" Canyon asked in return.

"You're here, O'Grady," Maxwell said. "There must be a body. Are you dirtying sheets again?"

Alison, wrapped in a towel, was holding a bedsheet against Canyon's fresh wound to staunch the flow of blood.

"I'd like to get him to the hospital without wasting time," she said angrily.

Canyon had asked Alison to send someone for the police, and she had called upon a neighbor to do so. A uniformed man had responded, soon followed by Inspector Maxwell.

"All in good time, Miss—"

"Gordon."

"Ah, yes," Maxwell said, "the nurse from the other night."

"The body's on the other side of the bed," Canyon said.

Maxwell walked over, lifted the sheet that was covering the body, and grunted.

"Do you know him?" Canyon asked.

"Of course. He goes—or went—by the name of Razor. He was a professional killer." Maxwell looked at Canyon. "This is the third such man you've killed since you arrived, Mr. O'Grady. Coincidence?"

"He broke in," Alison said. "He said he was . . . he was going to cut my—cut me, and Mr. O'Grady stopped him. That's all that happened here, Inspector. Now can we get him to the hospital?"

"That's how it happened, O'Grady?" Maxwell said.

"That's it." Canyon affirmed.

He flinched as Alison applied more pressure to his wound.

"Oh, dear," she said, "the other one has started to bleed a lot, too."

"All right," Maxwell said, giving in. "Get him dressed and we'll take him to the hospital."

Somewhere along the way to the hospital Canyon had either fallen asleep or passed out. When he woke up, he was lying in a hospital bed. He leaned to his side to take the pressure off his back.

"That's right," he heard Alison say. "This time we got you a bed."

He looked around and saw her approaching him. She was wearing her uniform.

"Are you all right?" he asked.

"Fine."

"Alison, I'm sorry."

"Canyon, I don't think I'm ready to talk about all of this yet."

"I'm sorry—"

"Your wounds have been tended to by a doctor this time," she went on, not giving him a chance to apologize. "I'm on duty, and I have to go to work."

"Alison—"

"Inspector Maxwell is outside," she said, heading for the door. "I'll send him in."

As Maxwell came into the room he said, "That's quite a girl. After what she's been through, she's working."

"Yeah."

"Think she's been scared off now?" the Inspector asked. "Maybe you'll have to find yourself another girl."

"Inspector," Canyon said, "get me my clothes, will you?"

"What for?"

"I'm leaving."

"No, you're not."

"Yes, I am."

"Look, why don't you play it smart for a change and stay put. I can protect you here."

"I don't need protection."

"How can you say that? If you had let me put a man on you before, this wouldn't have happened."

Canyon didn't reply, and a light dawned behind Inspector Maxwell's eyes.

"Ah, I get it. You want them to keep trying for you.

Why?'' He was talking to himself, so Canyon didn't interrupt. ''So you can kill them?''

''For your information,'' Canyon said, ''that fool shot himself.''

''And if he hadn't, you could have asked him who hired him,'' Maxwell said, ''or do you already know that? Yeah, maybe you know who hired the three of them, but you don't know where to find him. Is that it?''

''My clothes, Inspector.''

''Sure,'' Maxwell said this time, ''why not? It might not be such a bad idea to have you out there with a target painted on your back.''

He retrieved Canyon's clothing from a closet and tossed everything onto the bed.

''You know,'' he said, ''one way or another I'm going to find out what's going on, so why don't you just tell me?''

Canyon sat up in bed and busied himself with his clothes. Starting to dress, he took the time to evaluate the situation. As it was turning out, Postman and his people were not being much help. Maybe what he ought to do was level with Maxwell, and see if the policeman could help him at all. Of course, he still didn't have to tell him everything.

''Well?'' the impatient lawman asked.

Canyon took a moment, then said, ''All right,'' and told Maxwell what had happened to Locken in West Bend.

''So you came in his place,'' Maxwell said, ''and whoever wanted to kill him was trying to have you killed, thinking you're him.''

"Yes."

"And if he found out you weren't Locken?"

"It wouldn't make any difference," Canyon said. "I still want him, and he knows it."

"What's his name?" Maxwell said.

"All I know is that he's called the Duke."

"The Duke?" Maxwell said.

"Sound familiar?"

Maxwell shook his head. "He must not be from New York—and if he's not, why'd he come here?"

Because he's got something to sell, and figures this is the place to sell it, Canyon thought, but he didn't want to tell Maxwell that at the moment.

"Tell me about Razor," he asked the Inspector.

"What's to tell?"

"Was he for hire off the street, or would my man have had to make a contact?"

Maxwell's eyebrows went up.

"You are good, aren't you? You're quite right. Your man would have had to hire Razor through a contact."

"Like who?"

Maxwell was rubbing his jaw, and now he turned and headed for the door, grabbing Canyon's pants from the bed as he went.

"Like who, Inspector?" Canyon shouted. "And bring those back!"

"Get some rest," Maxwell said. "If you still want out in the morning I'll come and get you."

"Maxwell!" Canyon shouted again, but the policeman was gone.

12

When a knock sounded on his door the Duke looked up sharply, concern on his face. No one knew where he was staying except the woman who was lying next to him in bed, and she simply thought he was a man named Duke.

The woman stirred and said, "What's that?"

"Quiet," he told her, leaving the bed.

She watched him uneasily as he picked up his gun and approached the door. She'd have some questions after this, he knew.

He got to the door and waited until whoever was on the other side started knocking again, and when he whipped the door open. In the hall Armand Coles took a single step back, and then smiled at him.

"What the hell are you doing here?" the Duke demanded.

"I'm afraid I followed you," Coles said. "I am truly sorry, but my curiosity got the better of me."

"It may be the death of you," the Duke said coldly.

Coles frowned and said, "There's no need for threats, *mon ami*, I assure you. If you will let me in, I have a business proposition for you."

"Come inside," the Duke said, "and keep your hands where I can see them."

Coles entered and looked around. It was clear that there were two rooms, the one they were in and one other. He could see the doorway of the other room. He could also see the woman in the bed in this one.

"I am sorry to disturb you, miss," he said gallantly.

The woman sat up in bed and pulled the sheet up to her neck.

"Duke . . ." she said nervously.

"It's all right," the Duke assured her. "He's not staying long. Why don't you go into the other room."

She looked around and said, "My clothes . . ."

Impatiently the Duke said, "Just wrap the damn sheet around you."

The woman stood up, keeping herself covered as best she could, but Coles still caught sight of an expanse of solid thigh. She wrapped the sheet completely around herself and walked with as much dignity as she could muster into the other room, closing the door behind her.

"I could have got you a better-looking woman," Coles said, "although I must admit she does have a nice solid body. Her face, though—"

"Her face is fine," the Duke said. Gesturing with his gun, he added, "You'd better explain."

"It's very simple," Coles said. "I don't like to work in the dark."

"What's that mean?" the Duke said. "You work for Taylor, you do as you're told, right?"

"Wrong," Coles said. "I work for myself, although

I sometimes work *through* Taylor. Do you see the difference?"

"I see it."

"You really don't need that gun, you know."

"I'll hold onto it for a while."

"As you wish."

The Duke was naked, but he didn't want Coles to think that bothered him, so he stayed that way instead of grabbing a pair of pants. The Duke was still fairly new to this world, although he had trained himself for a long time to enter it. Up to now he thought he was doing very well for himself.

"All right," he said, "what's the business proposition?"

"First I must tell you that Razor is dead."

"What happened?" the Duke asked, surprised.

"He was killed by your man, O'Grady."

"How did that happen?"

"He found out where O'Grady's woman lived and he attacked them there. All I know is that Razor is the one who ended up dead."

The Duke thought a moment, biting the inside of his cheek, and then said, "O'Grady's good."

"Yes, obviously."

The Duke looked at Coles. "Were you there?"

"No," Coles said, "but I heard about it. I understand that O'Grady was wounded, though not very badly."

"If he's hurt, then he's set up for you," the Duke said. "You should be able to take him easy."

"I prefer not to think that way," Coles said. "I

always assume that my prey is healthy and intelligent. That way I am always at my best."

The Duke nodded. That made sense. It was something he'd have to remember.

"We need to renegotiate our deal, Mr. . . . uh, Duke."

"What are you talking about?"

"I need more information about this man O'Grady."

"Why?"

"The more I know about him, the better chance I have of killing him."

The Duke hesitated, then asked, "What do you need to know?"

"Who is he?"

"His name is O'Grady."

"Is that all you know about him?"

"He's after me," the Duke said. "I don't know much more than that."

"Why is he after you?"

The Duke shook his head.

"Come now," Coles said, "there is nothing you could tell me that would shock me."

The Duke shifted uncomfortably.

"Would you like to put some clothes on?"

"I'm fine."

"Shall I tell you what I think?"

"Go ahead."

"Do you still think you need the gun?"

The Duke hesitated again, then lowered the gun but kept it in his hand.

"You went to Taylor when you arrived in New York," Coles said. "Taylor's particular talent is selling things, so that would indicate that you have something to sell."

"And if I do, what does that mean to you?"

"It would mean a lot more to me if I was the one who put you together with a buyer."

"Are you offering to compete with Taylor?"

Coles shrugged and said, "Money is money. Why should you care where it comes from?"

"I don't think I'd be able to trust you."

Coles smiled. "And what makes you think you can trust Taylor?"

"I don't."

"Then there's no difference."

"Keep talking."

"Very well," Coles said, satisfied that he finally had the Duke's attention. "If I can find you a buyer, will you do business with me instead of with Taylor?"

"What would your take be?"

"Taylor takes twenty percent," Coles said. "Since I am trying to compete with him, I would take . . . fifteen."

"You'll need to take care of O'Grady first," the Duke said. "We're not going to be able to do anything with him around."

"What has he to do with what you're selling?"

"That's simple," the Duke said. "He doesn't want me to sell it."

"Is it his?"

"No," the Duke said, "it belongs to the people he works for."

"And will you tell me who they are?"

"No," the Duke said. "You don't need to know that."

Coles hesitated, then nodded and said, "You might be right about that."

"If you need help with O'Grady—"

"I will not need help," Coles interrupted. "I will take care of him myself. You accept my offer? Fifteen percent?"

"Fifteen percent."

"And what is it we are selling?"

"Let's just say that it is something with great . . . political implications. Will that help you in finding a buyer?"

"I will, but it will not help me in sewing one up for us."

"That part of it will be my job," the Duke said. "I'm prepared to make a pitch."

Coles took a moment to consider the form their deal was taking, then nodded.

"All right," he said, "I don't know everything I would like to know, but I think I know enough to get started."

"And getting started means taking care of O'Grady."

"Yes," Coles said. "I will let you know when that is done."

"Through Taylor?"

"Forget Taylor," Coles said. "This is now between you and me."

"Taylor might still get me a buyer."

"I'll worry about that."

"All right."

"Don't move from this location," Coles said. "I will tell no one about it."

"All right," the Duke said again.

Coles moved toward the door, then stopped before opening it.

"Would you like me to find you another woman?"

"No," the Duke said, "this one is fine."

Coles wrinkled his nose. "She smells of cooking grease."

"She's a waitress."

"Ah," Coles said, "that explains it."

After Coles left, closing the door behind him, the Duke went to the door, locked it, and then jammed a straight-backed chair beneath the doorknob. Only then did he put away his gun.

"Can I come out now?" the woman asked. Her name was Marcy, and her tone was contrite.

"Yes," the Duke said, "you can come out."

As she came into the room she asked, "Who was that horrible man?"

"Just a business acquaintance," the Duke said, sitting on the bed.

A business acquaintance he was probably going to have to kill.

Early the next morning Armand Coles was outside Taylor's Junk Shop. He watched as Taylor flipped the sign from CLOSED to OPEN and then waved Coles in.

Coles entered, closing the door behind him. Taylor's back was turned, so he didn't see the other man flip the sign back to CLOSED.

"Coles," Taylor said from behind the counter. "What can I do for you?"

"Did you hear about Razor?"

"I heard," Taylor said. "So?"

Coles shrugged. "I just thought you'd like to know."

"I would think you'd be more concerned with that information," Taylor said. He was shifting things around behind the counter. Coles wondered who would buy any of this junk from Taylor, because that was what it all looked like, junk. He knew that people bought it, though, because the shop was more than just a front.

"I don't know who this fella is who killed him," Taylor said, turning to face Coles, "but if you want me to get you some help to deal with him—"

"I'm not the one who needs help, Taylor," Coles said, cutting the other man off.

"What's that supposed to mean?" Taylor asked with a frown.

"It means," Coles said, "that I'll be making all my own deals from now on."

Taylor assumed a belligerent look.

"You think you can do better for yourself without me?"

Coles grinned. "I know I can."

"Fine," Taylor said, "go off on your own, then. Killers like you are a dime a dozen. If it takes me more than six minutes to replace you I'll retire."

He turned his back on Coles again and Coles took

a leather thong out of one of his jacket pockets. He had fashioned it into a loop before entering the shop.

"You'll retire now, Taylor," he said, and slipped the loop easily over Taylor's head.

13

When Canyon woke the next morning he was still angry with Maxwell for stealing his pants the night before. His wounds were sore, but still being in the hospital bothered him even more.

As if on cue a nurse walked in carrying his pants. She was older than Alison, in her forties, solidly built. Her hair was steel-gray.

"The Inspector asked me to give these to you this morning when you woke up," she said, laying the pants on the bed. "I guess that means you'll be leaving us this morning?"

"Just as soon as I can get them on," he said.

"I'll tell the doctor."

As she left he threw back the bed sheet and swung his feet to the floor. He felt a pull in the back wound and grimaced, sitting still for a moment. He tested the movements he could make, seeking the ones that would bring a minimum of pain or discomfort, then stood up and reached for his pants.

He had only one leg in when the doctor entered. He was a tall, slender man in his late fifties, and he gave Canyon a stern look.

"I understand you're leaving this morning?"

"Everyone understands perfectly," Canyon said.

"I wish you would change your mind."

"Why?"

"A cut like that can get infected very easily."

"I'll be careful."

"Mr. O'Grady—"

"I'm sorry, Doctor," Canyon said, "but I've got too many things to do to stay in a hospital bed any longer."

"The Inspector said you were stubborn."

"That may be the only thing the Inspector has been right about."

"I'm sure he'll be glad to hear that," the doctor said. "I understand he'll be coming to pick you up this morning."

Canyon looked at the doctor and asked, "How come everyone around here is so damned understanding?"

Canyon was dressed when Maxwell arrived, carrying Locken's knife and the .36 Colt.

"Ready to go?" he asked.

"I was ready last night."

"Sorry about that," Maxwell said, "but it really was best that you stayed here overnight."

Moving stiffly, Canyon took the knife and gun from Maxwell.

"In fact," Maxwell added, watching him move, "you probably should—"

"Don't say it," Canyon interrupted. "I've already heard enough for one morning. If you won't take me to my hotel, I'lll make my way there on my own."

"Oh, I'll take you," Maxwell said. "On the way I'll tell you how I started my day."

"How's that?"

"With a murder," Maxwell told him, and made him wait to hear the rest until they were in a coach, on the way to the hotel.

"Taylor's dead."

"Who's Taylor?"

"I keep forgetting you're not from here," Maxwell said. "I mean, you know so many people—"

"Who's Taylor?" Canyon asked again.

"We were checking on contacts your man may have made when he came to town," Maxwell said. "Taylor would have been one such contact. He's a fixer, a supplier, he could even be called an agent. He could get you almost anything you wanted in New York."

"And?"

"And somebody killed him," Maxwell said.

"How?"

"He was strangled with a leather loop. the thong was buried so deeply into the flesh of his neck that you couldn't see it."

"What's that mean to you? Or me?"

"Maybe nothing," Maxwell said. "Taylor dealt with a lot of dangerous people who might have killed him."

"Or he could have been killed by the person I'm after," Canyon continued.

"Yes."

"Why?"

"I don't know," the Inspector said. "I guess I'll have to ask him when I catch him."

The coach pulled up in front of the hotel. Maxwell got out first, then watched as Canyon stepped gingerly down to the street. It took only a moment for Canyon to spot the two men across the street.

"Yours?" he asked.

"For your protection."

"I don't think so."

"Oh? And why not?"

"I think you finally decided that I'm the best bait you have. I think you've got your men watching me to catch whoever tries to kill me next."

"It doesn't sound like such a bad idea," Maxwell said.

"It's fundamentally sound," Canyon agreed.

"Then what's wrong with it?" Maxwell asked.

"Nothing," O'Grady said, "only it may keep anyone from trying for me again."

"In which case you'll stay alive. It sounds to me like you can't lose either way."

"Oh, I lose," Canyon said. "I came here to find someone, and if I don't I lose." And so does the government, he thought, only he didn't say it out loud.

In the small cafe where Marcy worked, the Duke read over breakfast the account of Taylor's death—or rather, the discovery of his body. It didn't take a genius to figure out that Coles had decided to eliminate the competition rather than compete. Well, the Duke couldn't very well blame the man for that. He really didn't care one way or the other, as long as he got his buyer.

The Duke found this life—running from the government, having something dangerous to sell—invigorating, and he felt that he had prepared himself quite well for it. The only thing he hadn't done so far was any of his own killing.

He suspected that would soon change, courtesy of Armand Coles.

In front of the hotel Canyon decided that he was hungry. He and Maxwell walked to the little cafe where they'd had breakfast once before, the one Alison had introduced Canyon to. The same waitress was there. Canyon wondered if she worked all the time.

"You want another clean cup today?" she demanded of Maxwell.

"I'm sorry about what I said," Maxwell told her contritely. "Your cups are clean, and your food is excellent. And, of course, the service cannot be faulted."

Somewhat mollified, the waitress said, "Well . . . I'll get you your eggs."

She brought them a pot of coffee, poured them each a cup, and then left again. They both watched her walk away. She was solidly and attractively put together.

"All right," Canyon said, "tell me what you expect of me today."

"Just do what you want to do," Maxwell said. "My men will be right behind you."

"This isn't going to work."

"It has to," Maxwell said. "If the Duke wants you dead, he's going to have to try, whether my men are around or not. Of course, he'll send someone else to do it. There's no shortage of hired killers in New York."

"If you take your men off me," Canyon said, "maybe he'll make the try himself." .

"I doubt it," Maxwell said. "This sort of man rarely does his own killing when he can hire it out."

The waitress brought their breakfast, and Maxwell's plate was actually slightly fuller than Canyon's.

"I think she likes you," Canyon said.

"Haven't you noticed?" Maxwell replied. "Everyone likes me."

After breakfast Maxwell walked Canyon back to his hotel. The two policemen followed behind them. When they reached the hotel Canyon saw Billy Rosewood waiting out front, leaning against his cab. When Rosewood saw Maxewell he looked around as if seeking someplace to hide, but evidently decided there was no point.

"Good morning, Billy," Canyon said.

"Canyon," Billy said, and then as an aside he added, "Inspector."

"Billy."

"What happened to you this time?" Billy asked Canyon.

"I'll leave the Inspector to tell you that," Canyon said. "I want to go inside to my room and rest for a little while. I'll see you this afternoon, Billy."

As he walked toward the hotel door he heard Maxwell say, "Well, Billy, it's like this . . ."

Inside, Canyon collected his key and walked slowly to his room on the second floor. As he inserted the key into the lock he suddenly stopped, alerted by some instinct—an instinct he had learned to trust over the years. Given the problems of the last couple of days, it was an instinct he could easily have thought had deserted him.

He took out his gun, turned the key, and slammed the door open.

Alison, on the bed, sat up quickly, startled.

"Jesus," she said, "you scared me!"

"What are you doing here?"

"I knew you were leaving the hospital today," she said. She was sitting on his bed, but she was fully dressed. Her manner, however, made it clear that *that* condition was susceptible to change.

"I thought you might need a live-in nurse for a while," she said.

He closed the door and set the gun aside, within easy reach.

"After last night I didn't expect to see you again so soon."

"Neither did I."

"Changed your mind?"

"Yes," she said. "It was my choice to become involved with you. I can't blame only you for what happened—or what almost happened."

"I'm glad."

"You also changed your mind."

"How did I do that?"

"By making me like you," she said, and then added, "a lot."

"I like you, too, Alison."

"Here," she said, "let me help you off with your jacket and shirt, and you can lie down."

After she assisted him with his clothes she helped him into bed, where he lay first on his side, then on his belly, and then back on his side again.

"The doctor did an excellent job on your back," she said. "The dressing is nice and tight, and may pull a bit, but if you don't do anything violent, the wound shouldn't open again."

"Anything violent?" he asked, reaching out to touch her arm. "What did you have in mind?"

She smiled and reached for his pillows, propping them behind his back so that he was lying almost face up. She then reached for his pants and unbuckled them.

"Just lie still," she said, her voice growing thick, "and let me do it all."

She leaned over and kissed him, and her hands slid down inside his pants. She kissed his mouth, his cheeks, his chin, his chest, then slid his pants off and dropped them to the floor. She returned her mouth to him then, licking his nipples as she took hold of him, caressing him with both hands.

"Jesus, Alison—" he said.

Her tongue moved wetly over him, down across his belly, until she swooped down on him with her mouth, taking him deep inside.

"Oh, God . . ." he moaned.

Later she lay beside him naked, absently stroking his thigh with one hand. He was still lying with the pillows behind him, and lying still this way he felt hardly any discomfort from the wound. That would come, he knew, when he decided to move again.

"What are you going to do now?" she asked.

"About what?"

"You know what I mean. Are you going to keep looking for . . . for that man?"

"The Duke," Canyon said. He didn't remember if he'd ever mentioned the name in her presence or not. "He calls himself the Duke."

"It sounds silly," she said, "unless he's a real duke."

"He's not."

"If you don't find him soon," she said, "he'll send someone else to try to kill you, won't he?"

"Yes."

"And the police?"

"Inspector Maxwell has assigned two men to stay outside the hotel. They'll follow me wherever I go."

"That's good, isn't it?"

"That depends on how you look at it," Canyon said. "I'm of the opinion that not much is going to happen while they're out there. Of course, the good thing is they can look out for you."

"What do you mean?" she asked. "I'll be with you."

"No, Alison, you won't,"he said. "I need to get out of here, and without them."

"And what do you want me to do?"

"I want you to stay here, walk by the window a few times, act as if you're talking to me."

"You want me to make them think you're still here?" she asked.

"That's right. Can you do that?"

"Well, I can . . ." she said, "but I don't know that I want to. I mean—won't you get in trouble?"

"Oh, Maxwell will be upset with me," he said, "but if you mean actually get in trouble with the law, no. I don't have to agree to have his men with me at all times."

"What are you going to do, though?"

"I'm going to try and find the Duke," Canyon said, "or someone who knows where he is."

"And then what?"

"And then I'll deal with him."

"You mean kill him?"

"Maybe."

"You know," she said, "I still don't really know who you are or what you're doing or why you want to kill this man."

"Believe me, Alison," he said, "I would tell you everything if I could. The only thing I can tell you is that the Duke is responsible for the death of a friend of mine. He had him shot in the back."

"That's awful."

"That's the reason I originally started hunting for him, but he also has something very important that I have to retrieve," Canyon said. It sounded ludicrous to him, because he didn't know exactly what it was that the Duke had, just that it was some sort of information. "I may want to kill him, but I won't be able to do it until I find what he has and get it back."

"This all sounds very mysterious."

"I don't mean to," he said. "I'm sorry that you've gotten involved, but will you help me, Alison?"

She sat up in bed and looked at him.

"Of course I will, Canyon," she said. "That's what I came here to do, isn't it?"

He pulled her down to him and kissed her.

"Thanks. Now here's what I want you to do . . . ."

14

When Largo entered Postman's office he was surprised to find that the big man was not eating.

"Have you heard what happened?" Postman asked.

"I heard."

"It appears that someone has gone into business for himself," Postman said. "Which of Taylor's people would you suspect?"

"Well, since Razor's already dead," Jim Largo said, "I'd say it's Armand Coles."

"Coles," Postman repeated.

"Are you upset about Taylor?"

"Of course I am," Postman said.

"I didn't know you two were close."

"Don't be an ass," Postman said. "The man was a colleague. I can sympathize with what's happened to him. It could happen to me sometime as well."

"That's the chances you take when you deal with the people you deal with. I'm sure you've thought of going into business for yourself from time to time, Largo."

"Even if I did," Largo said, "that wouldn't mean I'd have to kill you."

"No, it wouldn't."

They stared at each other for a few moments, and

then Postman said, "Well, we both know that Taylor underpaid his people."

"Or simply cheated them."

"It could have been any of them," Postman said, "but I like your assessment. I think it was Cole, too."

"Do you want me to do something about Coles?"

"Why? Did you do anything about Razor?"

Postman knew that Largo had been outside Alison Gordon's building when Razor had broken in on her and Canyon O'Grady.

"No."

"Why not?"

"I didn't think O'Grady needed my help," Largo said. "As it turned out, I was right."

"Then why would I need you to do something about Armand Coles?"

"O'Grady's a little the worse for wear after the attempts on him," Largo said. "Nobody's succeeded, but they've each managed to take a piece out of him. That might just soften him up for Coles. I'm sure your friends in Washington wouldn't want anything to happen to O'Grady."

Postman stared at Largo.

"What do you know about my friends in Washington?" he asked. "And what makes you think they have anything to do with this?"

Largo shrugged. "I keep my eyes and ears open."

"Well, continue to keep your eyes open and on O'Grady," Postman said. "Who's watching him while you're here?"

"Jeffries."

"Well, get back there yourself."

"I'm not the only one watching him, you know."

"Has our friend the Inspector finally put a man on him?"

"Two."

"Well," Postman said, "I believe Mr. O'Grady will be able to shake them if he wants to. Just make sure he doesn't shake you."

"Not in my own city, he won't."

Postman didn't hear the comment. Something had occurred to him at that moment.

"Better yet," he said, "go and see O'Grady."

"And tell him what?"

"Warn him about Coles."

"All right."

"Tell him that the man is good."

"Is that all?"

"Yes," Postman said. "Once O'Grady has the name I think he'll be able to track Armand down."

"It'll be interesting when he does," Largo said.

"And you, my friend, should be right there to see it."

Largo left Postman's office and headed over to Canyon O'Grady's hotel. On the way he thought about Armand Coles going into business for himself. He hadn't thought the man was that smart. Largo had worked for Postman for three years and had done very well for himself, even had some money put aside. But there was something to be said for being your own boss.

Maybe it was something he should start giving some serious thought to.

* * *

Alison listened intently to Canyon's instructions twice, once while they lay together in bed, and then again while they were dressing.

"You're right about this bandage," Canyon said, "it's nice and tight. I can actually move."

"Just don't get into any fights," she said.

"I'll try my best."

"What do I do after you're gone?" she asked. "I mean, how long do I keep walking back and forth in front of the window?"

"I should only need half an hour's head start, Alison. After that you can just go back home or to work. I think I'd prefer you go to the hospital. There are more people there."

"Do you think someone else will come after me?"

"I hope not," he said. "I hope that fella Razor only came to your place because he followed me, and that it had nothing to do with you. Still, why don't you just stay at the hospital today until you hear from me."

"All right."

He took the .36 and dropped it into his pocket, then took his own .44 and slid it into his belt.

"You'd better get going now," he told her, walking her to the door. When he opened it they both stopped short, because Jim Largo was standing there.

"Whoa," Largo said. "Hope I'm not interrupting something."

"She was just leaving," Canyon said, easing Alison out the door, past Largo.

Largo watched her walk down the hall until she disappeared from sight down the stairs, then looked at Canyon.

"Can I come in?"

"Is there a good reason for your visit?"

"The best."

"Come on in," Canyon said. "I was on my way out."

"What I have to say won't take long."

Largo entered and Canyon closed the door.

"You've got company across the street," Largo said.

"The police," Canyon said. "They're protecting me."

"I have an apology to make."

"You do?"

"It's from the Postman."

"For what?"

"For not getting you this name earlier."

Canyon's ears perked up.

"What name?"

"Coles," Largo said. "Armand Coles. He's the killer who was hired to back up Razor."

"He didn't do a very good job."

"Actually, they work separately, it's just that they were both hired."

"By who?"

"Let's assume it's the man you're looking for."

"And who do they work for?"

"A man named Taylor," Largo said. "He was found dead this morning."

"I see," Canyon said. "Is all of this confirmed?"

"No," Largo said. "If you want confirmation, you'll have to get it from Armand Coles."

"Do you know Coles?"

"I know his rep."

"Am I going to be able to take him alive?"

"Not if he can help it."

"Do you have anything else for me?"

"No," Largo said, "that's it."

"Do you think you might be able to tell me where someone like Coles might go to get a drink?"

"Sure, I can help you with that," Largo said. "There's a saloon called the Bucket of Blood on the Bowery that serves that kind of trade. You might find him there. You might even be able to leave him a message."

"All right," Canyon said. "Tell the Postman I appreciate the information."

"Sure."

Largo turned and walked to the door, then stopped.

"I'm real interested in what happens when you and Coles come together."

"Why's that, Largo?"

"You're both pretty good."

"Should I be flattered?"

Largo thought a moment, then said, "Yeah, I'd say you should be. I haven't seen very many men I'd actually *say* are good."

"As good as you?"

Largo smiled and said, "Now, I'd never say that, O'Grady."

"Should I be looking over my shoulder for you, Largo?" Canyon asked. "I mean, when this is all over?"

"I don't have a beef with you."

"And I don't have one with you. Why don't we try to keep it that way?"

"Good luck," O'Grady," Largo said, opening the door. "I'll be around."

Maxwell's men saw Largo walk into the hotel, but then they saw a lot of people walk in. Largo didn't ring any bells with them. They also saw Alison walk out. She had been described to them, and they both admired her as she walked down the street.

Just a short while later they saw Largo leave, and thought nothing of it.

As Alison turned the corner she saw that Canyon's timing was perfect. Coming down the street was Billy Rosewood, driving his cab. She quickly waved him down and gave him Canyon's message. That done, she turned and walked back to the hotel.

Maxwell's men saw her return and enter the hotel again. They exchanged a glance, each commenting wordlessly on the way she looked and walked. They kept their eyes on the window of Canyon O'Grady's room, and shortly saw Alison appear in it. It appeared that she was speaking, probably to Canyon O'Grady, which satisfied both of them that he was still in his room.

Actually, by the time Alison returned to the room, Canyon had already left. He was waiting by the back door of the hotel, and was ready when Billy Rosewood pulled up in his cab.

"Good," Canyon said, approaching the cab, "Alison gave you my message."

"Why the back door?" Billy asked.

"I've got someplace I want to go, and I don't want to bring any policemen with me."

"Where we going?"

"Let's get away from here before we're spotted," Canyon said, "and then we can talk about that."

15

Tracy's Gun Shop was on Tenth Avenue, a hole in the wall close to the Hudson River. Rosewood stopped the cab right in front of it, hopped down, and waved at Canyon to join him.

"This is what you asked for," he said to the agent.

"Is this fella any good?"

"You said you wanted something special, right?"

"That's right."

"Well, this is the guy who can supply it to you," Rosewood said. "Come on, I'll introduce you."

After they had driven away from the hotel, Canyon had asked Rosewood if he knew of a reliable gunsmith who could do some special work. In reply to that request, Rosewood had brought him here.

Inside a man stood behind the counter of a small, cluttered store. He was very tall and thin, and despite the fact that it was barely noon, he looked as if he needed a shave.

"Bert," Rosewood said, "this is a friend of mine. His name's Canyon O'Grady. He needs some special work done. Canyon, this is Bert Christie, the best gunsmith in New York."

"Mr. O'Grady," Bert Christie said. "What kind of work did you have in mind?"

"I need a sawed-off shotgun," Canyon said, and proceeded to explain just how he wanted to carry it.

"You want to use that jacket?"

"Yes."

"Take it off, then."

Canyon removed the jacket and handed it across the counter to Christie, who noticed the way Canyon was moving.

"Looks like you might have already had some trouble," he commented.

"With your help, I'm looking to avoid any more."

"Well, it would be easier if you were heavier, but I think I can rig a holster inside this jacket—wait a minute." He looked at Canyon and said, "How much time do I have?"

"I need it yesterday."

"Can you pay?"

"Yes."

"Well?"

"Well enough."

Christie rubbed a hand over his jaw, and Canyon could hear dry skin scraping against whiskers.

"Come back in an hour—no, hour and a half. I'll be closed, but bang on the door."

"Come on," Rosewood said. "I know where we can spend that hour and a half."

"And some money, I'll bet," Canyon said.

He followed Rosewood to a saloon that was just half

a block away. He took a table while Rosewood got two beers from the bar.

"Once you've got your jacket rigged, where are we headed?" Rosewood asked.

"The Bowery."

"What's there?"

"You know a saloon called the Bucket of Blood?"

"Sure."

"That's where I want to go."

"Why?"

"Because the next guy who's going to try to kill me drinks there."

"And that's your reason to go there?" Rosewood asked. "Hell, you'll find lots of guys there who would kill you for as little as two bits."

"I'm only interested in one."

"Well, if you want to find him, I guess that's your idea of doin' it."

"What would your idea be?"

"Well, sir," Rosewood said, "I believe I'd give some serious thought to movin' to a new city—were it me somebody was tryin' to kill, that is."

"Billy, if you don't want to go there—"

"No, no, Canyon, I'll take you," Rosewood said. "You're payin' the freight."

"That reminds me," Canyon said, "I owe you some money already—"

"We've got time to settle up."

"You're an optimist."

"Well, if you go and get yourself killed at the Bucket

I believe I'll be in too much trouble with Inspector Maxwell to be spendin' any money."

"You won't be," Canyon said. "You're not coming in, you're just dropping me off."

"You got eyes in back of your head?"

"What's that mean?"

"In that place, two eyes just ain't enough to keep an eye on all the potential trouble you can get into. Hell, four might not even be enough, but four's all we got between us, so we might as well use 'em."

"You'll need this, then," Canyon said, taking the .36 from his pocket and passing it to Rosewood beneath the table.

"This is a small gun," Rosewood complained.

"Hey, it was good enough for me."

"You know," Rosewood said, "I had a feeling this thing was gonna be comin' back to me sooner or later. I think I would have preferred later—much later."

Largo had followed Canyon to Tracy's Gun Shop, which he knew well. He also used Bert Christie for special work. Christie knew Largo by sight, but did not know his name, nor did he know that Largo worked for Postman.

One of Postman's hard and fast rules when he agreed to take Largo on was that anonymity be maintained. It was only lately that Largo was beginning to chafe beneath that cloak.

Maybe Canyon O'Grady's search for a man called

the Duke, and Armand Coles' involvement, would be the setup Largo needed to cast off that cloak.

Maybe.

Canyon and Billy Rosewood had another beer each and then walked back to Tracy's Gun Shop.

"Why doesn't he change the name?" Canyon asked.

"If your brother started the business, would you change the name?"

"I see your point."

When they got to the shop the front door was locked, as Christie had said it would be. Rosewood banged on it for a while until the tall man came and opened it.

"Come in, come in," Christie said. He seemed to be very excited about something.

"Did you come up with something?" Canyon asked.

"Did I?" Christie said. "Come and see. Come into my workshop."

They followed Bert Christie into his workshop. The walls were covered with all kinds of guns of all ages, as well as other weapons.

"Quite a collection," Canyon said, eyeing a curved saber hanging on the wall.

"Thank you," Christie said. "I'm rather proud of it. Here, here is your jacket. Try it on."

Canyon let the man help him on with the jacket.

"Now look inside, on the left side."

"Why the left side?" Canyon asked. "I'm right-handed. I guess I should have told you that."

"I saw that when you gave me the gun," Christie said. "It doesn't matter. Look."

Canyon looked inside the jacket and saw not a holster, but two bands that were closed.

"They're light," he said.

"Clamshell," Christie said. "Strong but light. And they're on hinges."

"Hinges?" Canyon said. "What for?"

"Watch."

Christie picked up a sawed-off shotgun and, as Canyon held the jacket open, swung the bands open on their hinges, fitted the shotgun into them, then snapped them back into place. The shotgun now fit snugly into the bands.

"Not so light, now," Canyon said.

"Keeping it from being seen is going to be your problem. If you keep your arm over it and keep the weight from hanging, you should be all right."

"How do I get it out when I want it?"

"That's the beauty of this. Let the jacket go."

Canyon let it go and it closed. It hung badly from the weight of the gun, but if he kept his hand in the pocket he could keep the weight under control.

"Now reach for it with your right hand," Christie said, his eyes shining.

Canyon reached for the shotgun, and as his hand closed over it the two bands snapped open and the shotgun came free in his hand.

"You see?" Christie said. The look on his face could only be described as one of glee.

Canyon stared at the tall gunsmith, then fit the shotgun back into place and snapped the bands closed. When he went for the gun this time he did so faster. The hinges snapped the bands back and the shotgun seemed to leap free.

"You see how much easier it is for you to get it by reaching across to the left side?" Christie asked.

"Yes," Canyon said. "Even faster than if it was on my hip."

He put the gun back in place and snapped the hinges shut.

"That's amazing," he said.

"That's fast," Rosewood said.

"The hinges snap open as soon as you touch the gun, putting the slightest pressure on them, and yet they won't open accidentally. I can practically guarantee that."

"I can see you're as good as Billy said you were," Canyon told Christie.

"It's just something I've been toying with," the man said, looking embarrassed. "You've given me the chance to put it into practice."

"How much do I owe you?"

Christie quoted a price that surprised Canyon.

"That's too cheap."

"As I said," the tall man answered, "you've given me a chance to put something into practice. That's more valuable to me than money."

Canyon looked at Rosewood for a sign as to whether or not he should argue, and Rosewood shook his head.

Canyon paid Christie what he asked.

"Thank you," the tall man said.

"I should thank you."

"I don't think so."

"Why not?"

"Because wearing that rig will probably end up getting you killed."

"Why do you say that?"

"The only reason you could want a rig like that is if you were walking into a situation you weren't sure you were going to walk out of."

"And why is wearing this rig going to be what ends up getting me killed?"

"Without it maybe you wouldn't go ahead with what you're plannin'," Christie said, and then added, "or maybe I'm wrong about that."

"Maybe you are," Canyon said. He put out his hand and the gunsmith shook it. "I'm obliged to you for the work you've done, Mr. Christie."

"Let me know how it turns out," Christie said. "I'd be very interested to hear."

"I will," Canyon said. He looked at Rosewood. "Come on, Billy."

When Canyon and Rosewood came out of the shop, Jim Largo was across the street, out of sight. His sharp eyes picked up the heavy hang of Canyon's jacket.

It seemed that Canyon O'Grady was now ready to visit the Bucket of Blood.

16

"You don't have to do this, you know," Billy Rosewood said. "There are probably other ways you can go."

"Name one," Canyon said.

They were standing in front of the Bucket of Blood. Rosewood had stopped his cab farther down the street and they had walked the rest of the way.

"Billy, how much worse could this be than some places I've been to in San Francisco?" Canyon asked. "I mean, the Barbary Coast is pretty tough, too, you know."

"In San Francisco they shanghai you," Rosewood said. "Here they'll kill you."

"Let's go inside."

"Okay, but listen up first. You're not a regular, so leave the woman alone."

"All right."

"They're pretty aggressive, though, so do it without insulting them. Even the women in here carry knives."

"Jesus," Canyon said, and opened the door.

The first thing that hit him was the smoke. It was thick, most of it floating close to the ceiling, but tendrils of it coming down here and there because they had nowhere else to go.

After that it was the heat. It wasn't an oppressive heat, but it was the heat given off by having so many bodies in such a small space—not that the Bucket of Blood was small, as saloons went, but it was doing a landmark business at this time of day.

If Armand Coles was in here—even if Canyon knew what he looked like—it would be almost impossible to find him. Canyon had to hope that Coles would see him, and that seeing his target in one of his own drinking places would push the man's timetable up and make him move before he was ready to.

Canyon had entered first and went to find a spot at the bar. He had a beer in his hand when Rosewood came in a few minutes later. Canyon had to give the younger man credit. If he was scared, he certainly didn't show it. He found a spot at the bar farther down from Canyon and ordered a beer.

Looking around, Canyon saw that Rosewood had been right about the women. They were all young, simply but provocatively dressed, so that much of their breasts were showing—and they all seemed to have big breasts. It must be a requirement for the job.

The agent knew he was drawing curious glances—from the bartender and from several of the patrons—but he ignored them and simply looked around the room, occasionally sipping his beer. He figured that given the clientele, a strange face could always be the law, and that's what they were all trying to decide.

Rosewood was not drawing as much attention as Canyon was. Either Billy boy had been here before, or he simply didn't present the aura of physical danger that Canyon did.

Canyon sat at the bar for about twenty minutes before one of the women decided to give him a try. Actually, Canyon could see that it wasn't really her idea. She had been sitting on a man's lap when he leaned over and whispered in her ear. She looked up at the bar, saw Canyon, then nodded and got out of the man's lap.

The man was a big fella with a pot belly and a heavy beard. He could have been Postman's brother, but there was no food grease in his beard. Also, he hadn't nearly as much hair on his head as he had on his face, and his nose was bigger and redder than Postman's. Where Postman's vice was food, this man's was obviously whiskey.

The girl was a real beauty. She had long dark hair, hoop earrings, a wide mouth painted thickly red. She was wearing a blouse that fell way off her shoulders so that the upper slopes of her breasts and a lot of cleavage showed. The breasts were large and firm. Canyon found himself wondering what was holding the blouse up.

"Hello, stranger," she said, moving in close to him.

"Hello."

She pressed right up against him so that he could feel the heat of her and the pressure not only of her breasts but of her large nipples, which were hard. Her perfume was thick and heady and hung around her like a cloud.

"You're new here."

"Yes, I am."

"My name is Lola."

"Hello, Lola."

"Don't you have a name?"

"I do," Canyon said, "but I don't give it out at the drop of a hat."

She pouted, pushing out her lush lower lip. She was so close he could have bitten it, and was sorely tempted to do so.

"You're not very friendly."

"I'm sorry," he said. "I have other things on my mind."

"You're not a lawman, are you?"

"No, honey, I'm not a lawman."

"That's good," she said, "because this bunch would have you for lunch if you were."

"From the looks of them," Canyon said, "they might anyway."

"Not if you're nice to me," she said. She shifted around so she could press herself flat against him, and in doing so came into contact with the shotgun.

"Whoa," she said. "Mister, you're looking for trouble."

"Who's the man who sent you over here?"

Without turning to look at the bearded man she said, "His name is Mosca. They call him King Mosca."

"What'd he want to know?"

"Your name."

"He also wanted to see how I'd react if you pressed your gorgeous body up against me, right?"

"You're pretty smart," she said, then licked her lips and asked, "do you really think I'm gorgeous?"

"Absolutely."

"You're nice," she said. "It's too bad Mosca's gonna kill you."

"No, he's not," Canyon said. "You go back and tell Mosca I'd like to talk to him."

"About what?"

"That's between him and me, Lola. Just go and tell him, all right?"

"What's in it for me?"

Canyon took some money out of his pocket and pushed the bills down between her breasts. The valley there was warm and sweaty.

"I'll tell him."

"By the way," he said, grabbing her elbow.

"What?"

"You wear too much perfume," he said. "You don't need it. You'd smell fine without it."

"All sweaty?" she said, looking at him as if he were crazy.

He smiled. "Especially all sweaty."

"Mister," she said, "if Mosca doesn't have you for lunch, I just might."

She went over to Mosca's table, sat down in the big man's lap, and evidently gave him Canyon's message, because Mosca looked past her at Canyon and studied him. The big man had three other men sitting with him, and Canyon felt sure that if all three stood up right now, Bert Christie's contraption was going to get an instant tryout.

From where Canyon stood Mosca's eyes looked black, like two holes in his face rather than like eyes. They were expressionless as he studied Canyon, and then the big man said something to Lola and squeezed her ass. She got up and walked over to Canyon.

"Mosca's interested in you," she said.

"Good."

"So am I."

He smiled and said, "Even better."

"First Mosca, then me. Right?"

"Right."

"All right," she said. She took his hand and said, "Come with me."

As she led him to Mosca's table, Canyon sneaked a glance over at Rosewood, who looked at him and then at the ceiling, as if to say, "Now you went and did it!"

"You wouldn't tell Lola your name," Mosca said.

"There wasn't any reason to."

"Will you tell me?"

"Are you inviting me to sit with you?"

"Yes."

"Then I'll tell you my name."

Canyon had been thinking about this as he crossed the floor to Mosca's table. Should he use his real name or a phony one?

He decided that the time for playing someone else was past. Let Coles and everybody else know who they were coming after.

"My name's O'Grady."

"All right, Mr. O'Grady," Mosca said. "Have a seat."

There were only four chairs at the table and all of them were taken. Lola was sitting, but she was sitting in Mosca's lap again.

Canyon looked around and saw there were no available chairs to be pulled over from other tables.

"Doesn't seem to be a chair available," he said to Mosca.

"Pick one," Mosca said, indicating the other three occupied chairs at his table.

Canyon looked at the three seated men, each of whom looked more than willing to die for the chair he was sitting in—if Mosca gave the word.

"They're your men," Canyon said. "You pick the one you want to die over a chair."

Mosca stared at him for a few moments, then looked at one of his men and said, "Get up, Sykes."

The man named Sykes got up, and Canyon sat down.

"Why do you have a shotgun inside your jacket?" Mosca asked.

"I heard this was a rough place."

"And is it?"

"Not so far."

Mosca laughed, a great booming laugh that drew everyone's attention.

"You don't think this is a tough place, huh?"

"I said not so far."

"There ain't a man in here who wouldn't kill you if I gave the word."

"That might be so," Canyon said, "but you let me

get close enough so that if you did, you'd be the first to die. That tells me that you aren't about to give the word."

Mosca's black eyes studied Canyon, and then he said, "You're right about that. Why don't you tell me what you're doing here, O'Grady?"

"I'm looking for a man."

"Do you see him here?"

"I don't know," Canyon said. "I don't know what he looks like."

"You've never met him?"

"No."

"Then why the hell are you looking for him?"

"He's going to try and kill me."

"He is?" Mosca said, raising his bushy black eyebrows. "Now, why would he want to do that?"

"He's being paid to."

"By who?"

"By another man."

"Well," Mosca said, "that sure makes sense. It's a better reason than some of these rats need."

"His name's Coles."

"Whose name?"

"The man I'm looking for," Canyon said. "Armand Coles."

"The man who's gonna kill you?"

"That's right. He drinks here sometimes."

"That a fact?" Mosca said. "What's the other man's name? The one that done the hiring?"

"That's not your concern."

That was the first thing that Canyon had said that

seemed to upset Mosca. The big man leaned forward, causing Lola to fall off his lap and land with a thud on the floor.

"Jesus, Mosca—" she exclaimed.

"Shut up and take a walk!" Mosca growled at her.

Lola got to her feet, rubbing her amble posterior, and walked over to the bar.

"You come in here," Mosca said to Canyon, leaning on the table, "where you don't belong, and you tell me something ain't my concern?"

"That's what I said."

"You got a lot of guts."

"Do you know Coles?"

"Everybody knows Coles," Mosca said, "but nobody here knows you."

"What's that mean?"

"That means that if Coles was in here, and he made a move against you, he'd have a lot of backing and you'd have none."

"Guess that makes me kind of foolish, don't it?" Canyon said.

"Guess it does."

"So I guess I'll be leaving."

"If I say so, you will."

"If I don't," Canyon said, "you don't."

Mosca sat back in his chair and folded his hands over his belly.

"I said I knew Coles, not that I was ready to die for him. You can leave, just don't come back."

"I won't."

"And take your pup over there at the bar with you."

Canyon looked at Billy Rosewood and jerked his head toward the door. Rosewood moved away from the bar, walked to the door, and left the saloon.

"Now you."

"If you make a move against me, Mosca, I'll have to kill you."

"This is between you and Coles, O'Grady," Mosca said. "I said we knew him, but Armand Coles has no friends in here."

"Good enough," Canyon said.

He stood up, then looked over at Lola, who was leaning on the bar with both elbows, her impressive chest thrust forward.

"Maybe another time, Lola," he told her. As an afterthought he reached out with one hand and just let it glide over one of her heavy breasts. He could feel the hard nipple on his palm and his hand passed over it, and Lola closed her eyes and shivered.

She smiled at him then and winked, and Canyon backed toward the door, keeping his eye on Mosca. At the big man's slightest move he would pull his shotgun and blow the man's gut wide open—although he'd prefer to avoid that.

He stopped when his back hit the door.

"If Coles is here," he said out loud, "or if any of you ever see him, tell him to come at me from the front, and not from the back like a coward. You tell him that."

He reached behind him with his left hand, opened the door, and backed out.

17

Jim Largo couldn't help but be impressed with Canyon O'Grady.

Largo had managed to get to the Bucket of Blood ahead of him and had been seated at a back table when the big red-haired man entered. Largo had been to the Bucket before, and although he was not a regular, his presence raised no eyebrows. He had bought a beer, taken it to a back table, and then settled in to watch Canyon O'Grady work.

He admired the way the man had not rushed into anything but had waited for an opening, and then the way he had handled King Mosca. After Canyon O'Grady had left, Largo just sat there, shaking his head. Largo had never seen anyone handle Mosca the way Canyon O'Grady had. This was Mosca's place, and these were his people, and they would have torn Canyon O'Grady apart if the big bearded man had given the signal—only he hadn't. Instead, King Mosca had allowed Canyon O'Grady to walk out.

Canyon O'Grady would indeed make a formidable opponent—if and when Largo decided to look at him as such.

Largo finished his beer and left the Bucket of Blood.

He knew Armand Coles on sight, and he knew that Coles had not been in the saloon during Canyon O'Grady's visit. The word of O'Grady's challenge, however, would undoubtedly get back to Coles, who would not take kindly to being called a coward.

On the street Largo realized that this was the difference between Jim Largo and Armand Coles. Coles would let being called a coward bother him, and would have to try and prove to Canyon O'Grady—and everyone else who had heard the accusation—that he wasn't. Largo would never bend to that kind of pressure. Largo had pride, he had an ego, but he also had a cool head.

O'Grady was trying to force Coles into going after him before he was ready, and he would probably succeed.

The question was, which of them would survive the encounter?

For the first time since meeting him, Jim Largo was actually considering putting his money on Canyon O'Grady.

Armand Coles recognized the waitress who had served them their coffee and suddenly realized why the Duke had wanted to meet here. She was the same woman who had been in his room the other night. When Coles had shown up at the Duke's room that morning, the other man had insisted they go to the restaurant to eat. Now he knew why.

"I like it here," the Duke said, as if reading Coles' mind.

"Hey," Coles said, "it's up to you where you want to do your eating. I myself prefer a place with a little more class—both for eating, and for discussing important business matters."

"Never mind where we're talking," the Duke said. "Tell me why we had to meet and talk, at all."

"It's about your friend O'Grady."

"He's not my friend," the Duke said. "In fact, I've never even met him."

"That was just a figure of speech, *mon ami*."

The Duke was about to tell Coles that he wasn't his friend either, but he figured Coles was using a figure of speech this time as well.

"What about O'Grady?"

"What about your name?" Coles asked.

"What?"

"This Duke business," Cole said. "Why do you not tell me your real name?"

"Why do you sometimes speak with a French accent?" the Duke asked.

Coles smiled and said, "Your point is well taken. I suppose we all have our own walls that we hide behind."

"I'm not hiding," the Duke said.

"You are very touchy, my friend," Coles said, "and you don't have much of a sense of humor. You need a sense of humor in this world—all right," Coles said hastily as the Duke made a move to rise and leave, "all right, forget the sense of humor."

"We were talking about O'Grady."

"I'm going to kill him."

"Well, hell, that's what I'm paying you for."

"I need to know who might come after me after I've done it," Coles said.

"What do you mean?"

"I think you know what I mean . . . Duke," Coles said. "Who is O'Grady? Who does he work for? Who's going to come after me after I kill him?"

"I thought you were good," the Duke said. "Why are you worried about some unnamed person coming after you?"

"I'm alive," Coles said. "In my business, that means I'm good—but it also means I keep an edge, and I don't operate in the dark. I told you that already."

"Why have you decided to go after him immediately?"

"O'Grady challenged me."

"You spoke to him?" the Duke asked.

"Uh, no, he left me a message."

"Where?"

"At a saloon where I drink."

"He knew your name?"

"Yes."

"How?"

"I don't know," Coles said, "but I'm not exactly unknown in this city."

"Maybe too well known," the Duke said. "What do you want to do now?"

"I'm going to accept his challenge," Coles said, "but first I need an answer to my question. Who is he?"

"I don't know."

"All right," Coles said. "Who do you think he is?"

The Duke hesitated and then said, "He might be a government agent."

"An agent?" Coles asked. "What kind of agent?"

"Have you heard of the Secret Service?"

From the look on Coles' face the Duke assumed that he had indeed heard of it.

"I've heard stories . . . you mean there is such a thing? A Secret Service here in the United States?"

"Yes," the Duke said, "and it's *very* secret."

"I think I'm beginning to understand," Coles said. "You've got some information, don't you? About this very Secret Service. That is what you have to sell."

"Does that bother you?" the Duke asked. "Are you going to become patriotic on me now?"

"I am never patriotic when there is money involved," Coles said. "Besides, I really *am* from France. There is nothing for me to be patriotic about. You know, it's a funny thing."

"What is?"

"That you should be calling yourself a Duke."

"Why is that funny?"

"Because," Armand Coles said, "New York has its very own Duchess, and she just so happens to deal in secrets. . ."

As Canyon and Rosewood entered the hotel the big agent saw the two policemen assigned to him leaving. From the forlorn looks on their faces—and then the relieved looks when they saw him—he knew that they had checked his room, found it empty, and figured out what he'd done.

"Hello, boys," he said with a wave.

"Mr. O'Grady—" one of the policemen said, but Canyon cut him short.

"Look, fellas," he said, "I won't tell Maxwell if you won't, whataya say? After all, I'm back safe and sound, aren't I?"

The two policemen exchanged glances, and Canyon smiled at them and patted one on the back.

"That's it," he said. "Now why don't you fellas go back outside? Mr. Rosewood and I are going to have a drink in the bar. Come on, Billy."

"Do you think they'll tell Maxwell you slipped out?" Rosewood asked.

"No," Canyon said. "If they did, they'd have to admit that they lost me. I don't think they want to do that. I have the feeling Maxwell is not exactly the forgiving type."

"Where are we going to go now?" Rosewood asked.

"I haven't the faintest idea."

They were in Canyon's room, having left the bar after one beer.

"You just gonna wait for Coles to come after you?"

"I don't think I have long to wait, do you?" Canyon said. "I just have to make myself visible."

"So you want to ride around tomorrow?"

"Maybe walk around."

"That wouldn't be smart, would it?" Rosewood asked. "I mean, he could pick you off from a rooftop with a rifle, couldn't he?"

"He could," Canyon said, "but he won't."

"What makes you say that?"

"Because I challenged him in the Bucket of Blood," Canyon said. "I called him a coward. He's going to have to come right at me, Billy. Right straight at me, just to prove he's better than I am."

"And is he?"

"Well, we don't know that, do we?"

"What if he is?"

"If he is better," Canyon said, "then I'll have to hope I'm luckier."

"That's a pretty brave attitude," Rosewood said, "especially considering you've been wounded twice."

"I'm all right, Billy," Canyon said. "Stop worrying about me. You're worse than a mother hen."

"It's not a hen I'm thinking about," Rosewood said. "You're my goose with the golden eggs, and I don't want to lose you."

Canyon laughed and was about to say something when there was a knock at the door. He opened it, and Inspector Maxwell walked in.

"Don't you have some business somewhere, Billy?" Maxwell asked.

Rosewood looked at Canyon, who nodded.

"I guess I do," he said, moving toward the door. As he went through the doorway he turned as if to say something to Canyon, but Maxwell slammed the door in his face.

"You lost my men today."

"Did I?" Canyon asked. "I'll help you find them again."

"Don't get smart with me, damn it!" Maxwell said.

"I didn't think your men would 'fess up."

"They didn't," Maxwell said.

"Then how—oh, I get it. You've got another man watching them?"

Maxwell shrugged and said, "Just as backup. What were you doing at the Bucket of Blood?"

"Was I there?"

"Come on, O'Grady," Maxwell said. "My man saw you go inside."

Canyon frowned. Maxwell could be bluffing, but how would he know to bluff about the Bucket of Blood? No, he probably did have a third man watching the first two, and the third man had followed Canyon.

Maybe that wasn't right, either. If he had been followed, why was Maxwell asking about the Bucket of Blood, but not about Tracy's Gun Shop?"

Consistent, O'Grady, he thought. Careless right from beginning to end. That was what happened when you got emotional involved with an assignment.

"What were you looking for there?" Maxwell asked. "Or who?"

"Billy told me about the place," Canyon said. "I was curious."

"Mmm-hmm," Maxwell said, moving around the room. He stopped when he reached the straight-backed chair Canyon had hung his jacket on. The Inspector picked up the jacket, looked inside, and then set it back down.

"My man was right," he said. "Your jacket is hanging heavy—very heavy."

"I felt I needed a little extra firepower."

"If you're going to frequent places like the Bucket of Blood, I can understand how you'd feel that way," Maxwell said.

"It's just for self-defense, Inspector."

"O'Grady, if you're going to run away from me I can't help you."

"Or yourself, for that matter."

"We could help each other."

"Pull your men off me, Maxwell," Canyon said, "and I'll get our man within two days. That will help us both, won't it?"

"Two days?"

Canyon nodded.

"And if you're wrong," Maxwell asked, "and you show up dead?"

"You'll have the satisfaction of knowing that you were right."

Maxwell studied Canyon, giving his proposal serious consideration.

"All right," he finally said, "I'll go along with you. Two days, forty-eight hours, and that's all."

"That's all I'll need."

As Maxwell started for the door Canyon said, "Tell me something?"

"What?"

"How did you know I went to the Bucket of Blood?"

"One of my men saw you go in."

As Maxwell opened the door to leave Canyon asked, "How did you know to watch the place?"

Maxwell smiled. "O'Grady, I always have someone watching that place."

When Alison Gordon left the hospital to go home she did not see the man following her. She was thinking about Canyon O'Grady. Although he had told her to stay at the hospital, there were plenty of nurses on duty, and she couldn't see the sense in hanging around and doing nothing, so she decided to go home.

The man followed her all the way home, and when she stepped up to the building door to insert her key, he closed the gap between them and pressed against her.

"Wha—"

"Take it easy, miss," he man said. "I'm not going to hurt you."

"What do you want?"

"Go ahead and unlock the door. We can talk about what I want when we're inside."

"Who are you?"

"Inside," he said, pushing her against the door. Her only options were to open the door or be crushed up against it.

Once she opened it and they were in the hall he said, "Let's go upstairs."

At her apartment door he instructed her to unlock it, which she did. Once inside her apartment, he backed away and took a good look at her.

"I can see what O'Grady sees in you, Miss Gordon," he said. "You're very beautiful."

"Should I be flattered?" she asked, trying to hide the fact that she was very frightened.

"No," he said, "there's no need."

"What do you intend to do now?"

"Now we get comfortable," he said. "We're just going to wait."

18

Later that day Canyon decided it was once more time to leave the hotel. He and Rosewood had again gone to the hotel bar for a beer.

On the way out Rosewood asked, "Where are we going?"

"Let's go to the hospital," Canyon said. "I want to check and see if Alison is all right."

Rosewood drove his cab to the hospital and waited outside while Canyon went in to see Alison.

Inside the hospital Canyon asked for Alison and was told that she wasn't working that shift.

"I know she wasn't scheduled to work," he said, "but she told me that she'd be here."

"I'm sorry," the older nurse said, "but she went home."

"How long ago?"

"Maybe an hour."

"Thank you," Canyon said, and hurried back outside.

"What's wrong?" Rosewood asked.

"She went home," Canyon told him. "Let's get there fast. I have a bad feeling."

"You don't think—"

"Let's just get there!" Canyon said.

When they reached Alison's building, he was out of the cab even before it had stopped, and Rosewood hurriedly followed him.

Canyon opened the front door effortlessly and rushed up the stairs to Alison's door, his .44 in his hand. He left the shot gun inside his jacket. Rosewood came puffing up the stairs after him, the .36 held unsteadily in one hand. Canyon held a finger to his lips and motioned for Rosewood to flatten himself against the wall on the other side of the door.

"Either she's inside dead, and we're too late," he whispered, "or there's someone inside waiting for me."

"What do we do?"

"I go in," Canyon said, "and you stay here until I call you."

"But I—"

"Wait here!"

Canyon took a step back, then kicked the door open and charged into the apartment, keeping low. There were no shots, but he still cautiously looked left and right before signaling to Rosewood to enter.

"What's going on?" Rosewood asked.

"She's not here," Canyon said. "No one's here."

"That wasn't one of your choices."

"I know," Canyon said, "and neither is that."

"What?"

"That," Canyon said, pointing to the bed. There was a note on the pillow. It read:

O'Grady,
Central Park at nine P.M., Central Park South entrance.

Coles

"Why nine P.M.?" Rosewood asked.

"It'll be dark by then," Canyon pointed out. "He figures he knows the park and I don't."

"And that gives him an advantage."

"That's what he thinks."

"Isn't he right?"

Canyon looked at Rosewood and said, "No. Come on."

"Where?"

"Back to my hotel."

"Are we gonna bring in the police?"

"No, I don't want the police in this. They'll get Alison killed."

"We can wait in a saloon near the park," Rosewood said. "I know a place."

"All right," Canyon said, "let's go."

The saloon Rosewood picked was two blocks from the Central Park South entrance to the park.

"What's the park like in this area?" Canyon asked Rosewood.

"There are some paths, but it's mostly trees and foliage."

"Lighting?"

"No," Rosewood said, "not unless there's a full moon."

Canyon nursed the same beer while they waited in the saloon. He wanted his wits about him when he walked into the park.

"Time to go," he said.

"Want me to drive you?"

"It's only two blocks away."

"What do you want me to do, then?"

"Nothing," Canyon said, standing up. He took out some money and dropped it on the table. "Have another beer."

Rosewood's eyes widened when he saw how much money was on the table.

"That's too much for one beer."

"But not for everything you've done for me," Canyon said. "Thanks for all your help, Billy."

"You sound like you're not coming back."

"Let's be realistic," Canyon said with a smile. "There's always the possibility."

"We could still get the police—"

"No," Canyon said, "I have to do this myself. Take care, Billy. With some luck I'll see you in a little while."

Canyon walked the two blocks to the park and stopped in front of it. The chances were good that Coles was inside already, and could probably see Canyon from wherever he was. Rosewood had been right, there wasn't much lighting. But although the moon wasn't full, it gave off some light. He touched the .44 in his belt, just for a little reassurance. He also had Locken's knife in his pocket. He had left the bulky shotgun in Rosewood's cab.

He took a deep breath and entered the park.

From inside the park Armand Coles watched Canyon O'Grady enter. It would have been easy to pick him off from this vantage point, but that wasn't what Coles wanted. That wouldn't be accepting the man's challenge—and he definitely wanted to accept the challenge and shove it right down the man's throat.

Canyon heard Coles.

Armand Coles had been born and raised in the city, and had probably never been out of the city. He knew nothing about moving silently through the brush. He was making more noise than a small, inexperienced Indian boy would make—than a gang of Indian boys.

Canyon had known that challenging Coles, bruising his pride, would work, but he hadn't expected it to work this well.

He had him.

O'Grady was gone!

Suddenly, just like that, as the path curved out of Coles' view for just a second, the man had vanished.

Coles backtracked, tried to find him again, but it was no use. Had O'Grady changed his mind and run back out of the park? No, Coles would have heard him running.

"Damn it, O'Grady, where are you?" Coles said aloud.

"Right here, Coles," Canyon said from behind him.

Coles froze.

"How—"

"You should learn how to move through the brush, Coles," Canyon said. "You picked the one place to meet in this city where you'd be at a disadvantage instead of me."

"You son of a bitch," Coles said. "You challenged me."

"And you lost," Canyon said. He pressed the .44 into the small of Coles' back and said, "Just stand still." He patted the man down and removed a Colt .45 from a shoulder rig.

"Isn't this a little uncomfortable?" Canyon asked.

"I usually carry something small."

"This was for my benefit?"

"Yeah."

"Oh. I guess I should be flattered," Canyon said. He moved back three steps and replaced the .44 inside his jacket and then switched the .45 to his right hand. "I should be, but I'm not."

"Oh, and why is that?"

"Because I'm a little tired, a lot beat up, and very angry, and—" He stepped forward and brought the butt of the .45 down hard on the point of Coles' shoulder.

"Oh, Jesus!" Coles shouted.

Canyon lifted his foot and drove the heel into the back of Coles' right knee. The man staggered and went down, holding his shoulder.

"Where's the girl?"

"Listen, O'Grady—"

Canyon grabbed Coles' left wrist, pulled his arm straight behind him, and brought the .45 down on it hard. The sound of the bone breaking was sharp and loud, and Coles screamed.

"Where's the girl?"

"Jesus, my elbow—"

Canyon grabbed the broken arm and pulled it back even harder. Coles screamed again.

"You've got one broken arm, Coles," Canyon said. "You want to try for two?"

"I don't know—"

Canyon put the .45 next to Coles' left ear and fired it. Coles screamed.

"Jesus, I'm deaf!" he shouted.

"Okay," Canyon said, speaking into Coles' left ear, "you got a broken left arm, a bad right knee, and you're deaf in your left ear." He grabbed Coles' right arm, pulled it straight back, and said, "Let's start on the right side."

"No, wait," Coles said, gasping out the words. He was crying now. "Jesus, wait—"

"I'm not going to wait very long."

"Let me . . . let me get my breath!"

"Uh-uh," Canyon said. "I let you get your breath you might try to lie. Talk now, Coles." Canyon pulled tight on the arm. "Talk, or be a cripple for life."

"Okay, okay," Coles mumbled. Canyon released his arm and stepped back. In that moment Coles reached into his boot and came out with a knife. He lunged at Canyon, who squeezed the trigger of the .45 and blew the top of Coles' head off.

"Shit!" Canyon snapped.

He heard someone running and turned, holding the .45 out in front of him.

"Hey, wait—" Rosewood said, both hands held out in front of him. In his right hand he held the .36.

"Billy, I told you to—"

"I know, I know, stay out of it," Rosewood said. "What happened?" he said, looking down at Coles' body.

"He killed himself," Canyon said, sticking the .45 into his belt.

"He killed himself?"

"With stupidity," Canyon said. "Come on, let's get out of here."

When they came out of the park, Largo was standing there.

"Is Coles dead?" he asked.

"He's dead," Canyon said.

"You've got a big rep in the West, O'Grady?"

"Why?"

"I been thinking about going west. It would help if I went with a rep."

"Mine?"

"I was thinking about that."

"Well, don't," Canyon said. "Not tonight, Largo. I've got other things to do. Besides, killing me wouldn't do anything for anyone's rep, believe me."

"I know."

"Do you?"

Largo nodded.

"My guess is you do what you do, and nobody knows about it."

"Do you know where the girl is?"

"I know someone who does."

"Who?"

"If I tell you," Largo said, "will you meet me after? Just you and me?"

"What the hell is this, Largo?" Canyon said.

"I asked you a simple question."

"You want to die that bad, Largo?"

"Tough talk," Largo said. "Let's just say I'm . . . curious."

"Jesus," Canyon said with a sigh. "All right, Largo, let me try and save the girl's life, and then you name the time and place. How's that?"

"Suits me."

"Where are they?"

"I don't know," Largo said, "but you know that little restaurant you been eating in?"

"Yeah, so?"

"Your friend the Duke eats there, too," Largo said. "Wouldn't it be funny if the two of you had been there at the same time and not know it?"

"Is this for real, Largo?"

"Oh, yes," Largo said. "Postman put the word out, and this is what we heard. The Duke eats there, but he doesn't only eat there."

"What's that mean?"

"He usually leaves with one of the waitresses."

"Which one?"

"The one with the firm calves."

"All waitresses have firm calves."

Largo smiled and said, "Not like this one."

19

Canyon stood just inside the doorway of the cafe and looked at both waitresses. He'd been wrong. One of them had very thin legs, but the other one—the one who was friends with Alison—had nice, well-rounded legs with firm calves.

What had Alison said her name was?

"Marcy," he called.

She turned and smiled when she saw him.

"Hello," she said, approaching him. "Are you meeting Alison?"

"Alison's not available," he said.

"Oh?"

"She's with a man."

"Oh, I'm sorry—"

"His name is—" Canyon started to say, but then realized that he didn't know the Duke's real name. Instead he described the man to her.

"That's Duke," she said, "my Duke."

"And he has Alison."

"But—that's not possible," she said, frowning.

"Why not?"

"Well, he's—I mean, he and I—"

"Where is he, Marcy?"

"He can't be with Alison—"

"He not only is with Alison," Canyon said, "he's holding Alison."

"What do you mean 'holding' her?"

Canyon grabbed her by the shoulders. "Marcy, he's going to kill her."

"Why?"

"Because he wants me."

"What for?"

"He killed a friend of mine, had him shot in the back."

"That's not—"

"Look, Marcy," Canyon said in a gentler voice, "he wants you to tell me where he is, that's why he took Alison. Now tell me, before he kills her."

She stared at his chest for a few minutes, then gave him an address on Delancy Street.

"Thank you."

He ran outside and shouted the address to Rosewood.

"Do you know where that is?"

"Yep!"

"Let's get there—fast!"

They made the trip in record time. Canyon had Rosewood stop the cab down the block from the building and they both got down.

"Stay here!" Canyon said.

"O'Grady—"

"This time I mean it, Billy!" he said sharply. "Stay here."

"All right."

Canyon walked away from the cab and started

checking the numbers on the buildings. When he found the one he wanted, he tried the door and found it open.

The Duke was really waiting for him.

He pulled his .44 out of his belt and went inside. The shotgun was back, clipped inside his jacket. The .45 he'd left with Rosewood.

Marcy had said that her Duke's rooms were on the second floor. This building was a lot like Alison's, and Marcy had said that the apartment was in the back.

Canyon climbed the stairs, winced as they creaked. When he reached the second floor he walked to the back. He was about to try the door when he heard a noise from above. It sounded like more than one person going up the stairs. He stopped and listened.

"O'Grady!" a voice called from above.

He didn't answer.

"I know you're there, O'Grady! I've been waiting for you." There was a moment's silence and then the voice said. "*We've* been waiting for you."

There was another moment's silence, and then Canyon heard Alison cry out in pain.

"Come on up, O'Grady," the man's voice said. "To the roof. We're waiting—but don't keep me waiting too long."

If he rushed up there he'd get Alison killed, for sure, Canyon thought. He had only seconds to decide how to play this.

The Duke—whose real name, Alan Mills, was of no consequence to anyone, not even himself—was at once angry and anxious—no, eager. He was angry because he had spent money on killers who hadn't been able to stop this man O'Grady. He was eager because all he had to do was kill O'Grady, and then keep his appointment with Armand Coles' mysterious Duchess. Coles had spoken to the woman—who he said was very beautiful—and she had expressed interest in buying information about the American Secret Service.

As Alan Mills, the Duke had been a low-level employee of the Secret Service, deemed unfit for the kind of service Locken and O'Grady provided. Well, Alan Mills had got tired of performing menial clerical tasks, and had decided to sell what he knew about the Service to the highest bidder. Upon arriving in New York, however, he'd found that many people did not believe in the Secret Service. They thought it a myth, and so there were no high bidders. In point of fact, this Duchess that Armand Coles had told him about was the only person to express concrete interest in paying for the information.

In preparation for his new life as the Duke, Mills had practiced with a gun until his hand hurt, and had studied hand-to-hand combat. Now it was time for him to put all of that to work. He had to get rid of Canyon O'Grady, kill the girl, then meet with the Duchess and make his sale.

O'Grady had probably done him one favor and killed Armand Coles, or he wouldn't be here now. The rest was up to the Duke, himself. Once he killed O'Grady he could claim responsibility for killing two Secret Service agents—this after the Service had refused to make *him* an agent, as he deserved to be.

Canyon started for the stairs that led to the roof, then paused and went to the door of the Duke's rooms. It was open and he went inside. He took a quick look around and then went to the window and opened it. He looked outside and saw a ladder attached to the side of the building. Rosewood had pointed this out to him on other buildings around the city. He'd said they were for quick escape in case of a fire. This one reached all the way from the ground to the roof.

Canyon tucked the .44 into his belt, climbed out the window, and stepped onto the ladder. The shotgun weight inside his jacket was unwieldy, and he took a moment to settle himself before starting to ascend. He hoped that the Duke would be expecting him to use the stairs.

The building was three stories high, and Canyon had been three stories high once or twice before—but never on a ladder attached to the side of a building. He hoped that it was securely affixed and would not come loose, dumping him onto the street below.

Finally he reached up and gripped the ledge of the roof. He pulled himself up until he was standing on the top rung of the ladder. From that position he could see the Duke, who was holding Alison tightly around the waist with his left arm and holding a gun in his right hand. As Canyon had hoped, the Duke was waiting for him to come through the stairway door to the roof.

Canyon was holding onto the roof ledge with both hands, and suddenly found that he was not particularly anxious to release it, even with one hand. Rather than grab for the .44 from his precarious perch, he hoped to be able to climb up onto the roof without being seen.

He jammed the toe of one boot into the side of the building where bricks had come loose and reached over with one hand for the inside of the ledge, while continuing to hold fast to the outside with the other hand. He pulled himself up onto the ledge, so that he was now hanging half on and half off the roof. He was thrown off balance, though, as the shotgun inside his jacket suddenly came loose and tumbled three stories to the ground. Had it happened just seconds earlier he might have gone right after it. He was going to have to tell Christie that his clamshells didn't hold under extreme pressure.

In this position, half on and half off the roof, he was helpless if the Duke turned around at that moment. He pulled and lifted one of his legs, getting the knee up onto the ledge. As he got the leg completely over, so that he now had one foot planted on the rooftop, the Duke suddenly turned his head and looked behind him. Whether the man had felt his presence or not, the Duke's mouth gaped open as he saw Canyon O'Grady, and he quickly turned all the way, covering the Secret Service agent with his gun. He still held a mute, white-faced Alison tightly with his left arm.

Canyon didn't know quite what he had expected the Duke to look like, but he found himself facing a very ordinary, unremarkable man.

The Duke fired once, almost accidentally, his finger jerking spasmodically on the trigger of his gun. The shot went wild as Canyon pulled himself up hard and fell onto the rooftop.

"Hold it right there, O'Grady!" the Duke shouted, pointing his gun. He didn't look like a man who was comfortable handling guns.

Crouched on the roof, terribly exposed, Canyon waited for the man to fire again.

"You are O'Grady, aren't you?" the man asked.

"That's right."

The Duke extended the gun further, stiffening his arm, using the gun to point rather than threaten, and said, "You have caused me a lot of trouble."

"I'm sorry."

"Hah!" the Duke said. "I'm sure you are not—but you soon will be. Take that gun out of your belt carefully and toss it away from you."

Canyon did as he was told, but did not toss the gun as far as he might have.

"You've kept me from making my deal in this city," the man said, "the deal I came here to make. Well, I'll take care of you tonight, and this girl, and then I'll make my deal."

"And what deal is that?"

"Don't you know?"

"Suppose you tell me before you kill me," Canyon said. "Surely you're not afraid to tell me?"

"I'll tell you, but not because you goaded me with that remark about being frightened. I'll be selling everything I know about your precious Secret Service, O'Grady. When the word gets out, the government's going to have a lot of explaining to do about the money they spend, about the things they do in secret. Your precious Secret Service will be no more.''

''I don't understand. Why would you want to do that?'' Canyon asked.

''Because,'' the Duke said, ''they kept me from being what you are and what Locken was, they kept Alan Mills from being the Secret Service agent he should have been.''

Canyon frowned.

''Is that you?'' he asked. ''Are you Alan Mills?''

An odd look came over the other man's face.

''Alan Mills is dead!'' he said. ''The Duke is here, and it is the Duke who will make the Secret Service pay.''

''Before you can do that, you're going to have to kill me.''

''That's what I intend to do,'' Mills said. ''Move to the edge of the roof, O'Grady.''

''Why?''

''Because you're going over.''

''Have you ever killed anyone before, Alan?''

''Don't call me that!'' Mills shouted, and Canyon could now see the madness in the man's eyes. If he hadn't killed before, Canyon believed that he could do so now. ''Alan Mills is dead. I told you that!'' Mills shouted again.

''I'm not going over the edge, Mills, or Duke, or whatever you want to call yourself,'' Canyon said. ''If you really want me dead you're going to have to kill me yourself.''

''Then I will,'' Mills said. He pushed Alison away

from him so that she stumbled and fell, and then pointed the gun at Canyon.

At that moment the Secret Service agent knew that Alison was going to try something, and he shouted, "No!" But it was too late.

As she stood up, her hands like claws, Mills turned and fired at her once. Canyon heard the bullet strike her and watched as she was thrown to the rooftop, and then he was moving. He dove for the .44. Had he kicked it farther away from him he never would have made it. His right hand closed on the grip and he came up onto his knees, swinging the gun around to point it at Mills. Alan Mills looked away from the fallen woman and saw Canyon moving. Desperately he started to bring the gun to bear on the agent, and both men fired their weapons at the same time.

Canyon felt Mills' bullet strike him on the side, felt it go in and out, while his own bullet struck Mills in the chest. The man's mouth opened as if he wanted to speak, but instead it began leaking blood. His gun fell from his nerveless fingers, and the man toppled over, falling right next to Alison Gordon.

20

A month later Billy Rosewood drove Canyon O'Grady to the railroad station where he would catch a train to Washington, D.C. It had taken that long for Canyon to recover completely from his various wounds. Also, he hadn't wanted to leave until Alison Gordon had also fully recovered.

"I thought maybe you'd started to like this city," Rosewood said at the station, "and maybe you'd stay around for a while."

"I do like it, Billy," Canyon said, "but I can't stay. I've got to get back to work."

"Whatever that is, right?" Rosewood asked.

Canyon smiled. "Right."

"I also thought maybe the lady . . ."

"Would what? Keep me here? Come with me?" Canyon shook his head. "I'm not quite ready for that kind of relationship, Billy."

"Still got too much movin' around to do, huh?"

"Something like that."

General Wheeler had been sending Canyon telegraph messages every week. He was eager to have Canyon back in Washington so he could get a complete report on Alan Mills, alias the Duke. Canyon knew that

Wheeler would want assurances that Mills hadn't had a chance to tell what he knew to anyone. Those were assurances that Canyon would not be able to give. The agent only had Mills' word that he hadn't yet sold his information to the mysterious Duchess he had mentioned. It would be Canyon's advice to Wheeler that the Secret Service do some housecleaning, some reorganization, just in case.

"How is the lady?" Rosewood asked as he took Canyon's gear down from the top of the cab.

"She's fine," Canyon said, thinking back to the night before and to this morning, "just fine . . ."

They had started making love even before their wounds were completely healed, but gently, ever so gently. It was only on that last night that they were able to have sex with the abandon they had both been wanting for so long.

The first time she had straddled him, staring down at him while she rode him, her hair wild, her teeth digging into her lips, her nostrils flaring, her head flung back as her time neared. He took her breasts in his hands, then slid his hands around behind her, down her smooth back until he could cup her buttocks. She moaned and lay flat on him, her hips still in motion, their flesh making moist slapping sounds as they moved faster and faster together . . .

. . . and still later he took her from behind, holding her hips in his hands as she crouched on her elbows and knees. Every time he drove into her he could hear her breath catch in her throat, and once or twice she would reach for him, groping behind her in her frenzy, and then she simply gathered the sheets in her fists, crying out, almost pulling the sheets completely from the bed . . .

. . . and then, when morning came, they made love again slowly, sweetly, because they both knew it was the last time. They explored each other's body with hands and mouths, as if memorizing every inch, and when he entered her he did it so slowly that it was almost painful. When he was finally fitted into her completely she wrapped him in her arms and legs and they moved together that way. They went slowly, wanting to make it last, and wanting to make sure they could remember every moment of it afterward.

She cried, tears streaming down her face, saying his name over and over as they rocked together, "Canyon . . . Canyon . . . Canyon . . ." and as their pace quickened she could no longer utter his name, but instead simply grunted or groaned as he slammed into her, and then finally exploded inside her . . .

Later, while she watched him dress, he said, "I'm sorry."

"About what?"

He leaned over and touched the puckered scar tissue on the upper slope of her right breast. She covered his hand with hers.

"It wasn't your fault," she said.

"Sure it was. I got you involved in the whole mess, all because I was attracted to you. If I had stayed away from you—"

"I probably would have come looking for you," she

said, cutting him off. "I'm not sorry for that."

"No," he said, "I'm not sorry for that either."

"Then don't be sorry for any of it," she said, taking his hand and kissing it. There were tears in her eyes when he left, but he knew they'd dry.

It was his experience that tears always did. . . .

"Whatever happened to that other fella?" Rosewood asked.

"What fella?"

"That Largo fella," Rosewood said. "Remember? You was supposed to meet him?"

"Oh, that," Canyon said, "He never showed up. I guess he changed his mind."

What had actually happened was that Largo sent Canyon a message while he was in the hospital. It arrived on the day he was getting out, and it told him where and when to meet Largo. Only when Canyon got there, Largo was nowhere to be seen. The only other person present was Postman.

"What are you doing here?" Canyon asked.

"I heard Largo was supposed to meet you here," Postman said.

"And?"

"I didn't approve of this, O'Grady," Postman said. "I can't afford to have my Washington, D.C. contacts angry with me, so Largo won't be showing up."

"Were you afraid that he'd kill me or I'd kill him?" Canyon asked.

"That," Postman said, "sounds like the kind of question Largo would ask."

Canyon smiled. "You're right."

"Have a safe trip back to Washington," Postman said. "Give my regards to Rufus."

"Uh-oh," Rosewood said.

"What?" Canyon asked, coming out of his reverie. He'd been daydreaming about Alison already, even while they walked to his train.

"You got company come to say good-bye."

Canyon looked around and saw Inspector Maxwell approaching them. He put his grip down and waited for the man to reach them rather than boarding the train, which was ready to leave.

"Inspector," he said, as Maxwell joined them, "how nice of you to come and see me off."

"I came to make damn sure you didn't miss your train, O'Grady," Maxwell said good-naturedly. "Things have been very lively in New York since you arrived. I don't know who you really are, or why you were really here, and I don't think I ever will, but I do know that I'm not sorry to see you go." The policeman extended his hand awkwardly and added. "Er, no offense meant."

Canyon smiled and said as they shook hands. "None taken, Inspector. None taken."